"All done," he said in a voice that was rougher than he'd intended.

When he handed the clipboard back to her, he was careful to extend his arm fully, rather than leaning in again. Then he tried to find something—anything—to stare at rather than the way she ran the end of her pen back and forth across her bottom lip.

She frowned and tapped the lucky pen on the paper, in the area where he'd filled in his current address. "That's a bit of a commute."

"About forty minutes," he said.

She frowned. "You're going to ride a bike back and forth?"

"Oh, a motorcycle kind of bike, not a ten-speed. My Harley." She laughed—a low, self-deprecating chuckle—and he wanted to hear more of it.

There was nothing sexier to Riley than a smart woman with a great sense of humor, and he got the impression Laura laughed a lot.

He was in so much trouble.

Dear Reader,

When I started working on the Sutton's Place series, I had no idea I'd end up writing a happily-ever-after for Laura Thompson. Her son, Lane, fell in love for the second time in *Expecting Her Ex's Baby*, and now it's his mom's turn to find romance. She never expects to fall for a younger man her son just hired to work for the family business.

The connections in a close-knit community can be complicated, and Riley McLaughlin finds that out the hard way when he tries to resist the chemistry sizzling between him and his new boss's mom. He fails, but their relationship could shake up their friends and family if the news gets out. It's not easy to keep a secret in a small town!

You can find out what I'm up to and keep up with book news on my website, www.shannonstacey.com, where you'll find the latest information, as well as a link to sign up for my newsletter. I love connecting with readers, so you'll also find links to where I can be found on social media.

Welcome back to Sutton's Place, and happy reading!

Shannon

Her Younger Man

SHANNON STACEY

HARLEQUIN
SPECIAL
EDITION

Recycling programs for this product may not exist in your area.

ISBN-13: 978-1-335-59418-1

Her Younger Man

Copyright © 2023 by Shannon Stacey

All rights reserved. No part of this book may be used or reproduced in any manner whatsoever without written permission except in the case of brief quotations embodied in critical articles and reviews.

This is a work of fiction. Names, characters, places and incidents are either the product of the author's imagination or are used fictitiously. Any resemblance to actual persons, living or dead, businesses, companies, events or locales is entirely coincidental.

For questions and comments about the quality of this book, please contact us at CustomerService@Harlequin.com.

Harlequin Enterprises ULC
22 Adelaide St. West, 41st Floor
Toronto, Ontario M5H 4E3, Canada
www.Harlequin.com

Printed in U.S.A.

A *New York Times* and *USA TODAY* bestselling author of over forty romances, **Shannon Stacey** grew up in a military family and lived in many places before landing in a small New Hampshire town where she has resided with her husband and two sons for over twenty years. Her favorite activities are reading and writing with her dogs at her side. She also loves coffee, Boston sports and watching too much TV. You can learn more about her books at www.shannonstacey.com.

Books by Shannon Stacey

Harlequin Special Edition

Sutton's Place

Her Hometown Man
An Unexpected Cowboy
Expecting Her Ex's Baby
Falling for His Fake Girlfriend

Blackberry Bay

More than Neighbors
Their Christmas Baby Contract
The Home They Built

Carina Press

Boston Fire

Heat Exchange
Controlled Burn
Fully Ignited
Hot Response
Under Control
Flare Up

Visit the Author Profile page
at Harlequin.com for more titles.

For J. Thanks for being my Lucy.
(It'll make sense after you read the book.) (Maybe.)

Chapter One

Happy Monday, Stonefield! We're halfway through July and everybody's tired of hearing "Is it hot enough for you?" because the answer will almost always be yes. (Except for the people who are about to comment that they wish it was hotter and our postmaster, who was stationed in Yuma in his twenties and has some stories about heat.) Town Hall has been fielding complaints about the grass drying and turning brown in the town square. They suggest you take it up with the people who complained about the cost of running the sprinklers. Stay cool, Stonefield!

—Stonefield Gazette *Facebook Page*

Having the hots for his new boss's mother wasn't a problem Riley McLaughlin ever thought he'd have in life, but here he was.

He'd only known Laura Thompson for five minutes and he was already…enraptured. It was a strange word he would have bet would never pop into his head, but he was taken with her and that was the only word he could think of.

It had been instant, too. Lane Thompson—one of the two owners of D&T Tree Service, along with his cousin Case Danforth—had shown him around the industrial garage and dirt parking area they called "the pit" before leading him up to the house.

"We have an office," Lane told him as they walked, "but it's not a *real* office, like open to the public. My mom runs the company out of her home office, though locals stop in sometimes, rather than calling. But it's also our house, so at first if you need something in the office, it's best to call or text first. You'll have more interaction with her than the other guys do since you're coming in as the lead foreman, though, so eventually you'll probably just go in and out like Case and I do."

"Okay. And your wife works in the office, too?"

"Sometimes, if my mom needs to be out." Lane chuckled. "Evie's been helping *her* mom out at the family thrift store since her sister had a baby. And she works in the taproom and handles the social media for all of those businesses, so she's pretty busy.

We're also newlyweds for the second time and we have a six-month-old baby. She's pretty busy."

"Wait. You're newlyweds for the second time?" Of course it was possible to be a newlywed more than once, but the *we* in that context tripped him up.

"We married and divorced young, and then she left town. Luckily, when she came home to help open Sutton's Place after her dad died, we figured it out. Forever this time."

"Congratulations on figuring it out, and for the baby."

"Thanks. Anyway, you'll run into Evie in the office, but she'll probably just tell you to come back when Mom's around. Don't take it personally."

Riley nodded as they climbed the porch steps, giving himself a moment to file that info away in his mind. Most of it he already knew, since it had come up when they met at Sutton's Place Brewery & Tavern for an informal interview. He knew he was being brought in because Lane was the head brewer and part owner of the brewery—along with some of his family—and had a new baby. Plus, Case had recently married Evie's sister Gwen, and they wanted to start a family. They had a lot going on and didn't want the tree service to suffer, so Riley was going to make sure that didn't happen. He'd pick up any slack, run the crews and be the go-to guy they could trust with the business they'd inherited from their fathers.

It felt weird walking into somebody's home, and Riley thought it would be a long time before he was comfortable just walking in to get to the office his boss led him to. Lane knocked twice on the doorjamb before stepping through the open door. Riley followed and stepped out from behind Lane just as the woman at the desk spun her chair to face them.

The woman's hair was dark, with deep shades of brown shot through with gray. It was piled on her head in a very messy knot, and her dark eyes lit up when she saw her visitor was her son. The laugh lines around her eyes deepened as she smiled, and then she turned that gaze on Riley.

"You must be the new guy," she said in a warm voice. "Come in and have a seat."

"This is my mom," Lane said. "She handles the office, and she'll get you set up with paperwork and anything else you need."

"Laura," she said, giving her son an admonishing look before turning back to Riley. "My name is actually Laura Thompson, not *Lane's mom*, but you can call me Laura."

Riley thought it might be best if he kept calling her *Lane's mom* in his head, even if he couldn't say it out loud. "It's nice to meet you, Laura."

Before sitting in the armchair she gestured to, he paused to shake her hand. One, it was the polite thing to do, and two, he wanted the brief physical contact to assure him he felt nothing. Sure, he'd always had a thing for dark-haired women with gorgeous smiles, but he'd just met this one.

But her hand lingered in his for a few seconds too

long, and he was close enough to inhale the fresh, slightly citrusy scent of her before he sat in the chair. He set the bottle of water he'd been carrying on the floor next to his foot.

"I'll leave you two to the paperwork," Lane said. "Come on out to the garage when you're done, and I'll find you a spot to stow your stuff."

And just like that, he was alone with Laura—*Lane's mom*, he told himself again—and he leaned back in the chair while she sifted through papers. He noticed a framed photo on her desk, and he had to squint a little to make it out. Based on Lane's younger appearance, it was an older family photo, and he found himself leaning in slightly to see Laura and the man he assumed was Lane's dad. Lane had told him a little about the company during the interview, so he knew that Joe Thompson had died about a decade ago, and Case's dad had died a few years later—leaving the company to be run by the two cousins.

"That was taken right after Lane and Evie got married," Laura said, and he was embarrassed to have been caught staring. "The first time."

Riley didn't admit he'd barely noticed Lane and Evie. "It's a great picture."

She nodded. "It's always been my favorite picture. For too many years, I had a version of it with Evie cropped out in the frame, but I'm glad to have the original back again, the way it was meant to be."

After she found the papers she was looking for, she put them and a pen on a clipboard and held them out to him. Leaning forward to take the clipboard from her put him close to her again, and he had to force himself to focus on the instructions she was giving him instead of the way being this close to her made him want to be even closer.

The forms were the standard kinds for any job, along with some extras pertaining to insurance and safety and all manner of things. It took him a while to fill them all out, especially since his senses wanted to stay tuned in to what Laura was doing.

She'd turned back to her computer after handing him the forms, enabling him to peek at her through the corner of his eye without her noticing. She was wearing a long floral blouse made out of some kind of flimsy material over a pink tank top, and pink capri-length pants. Her sandals showed off toenails that were a glittery hot pink, which made him smile.

When Laura turned, as if she'd sensed him staring at her feet, Riley cleared his throat and forced his attention back to the form he was supposed to be filling out. The only thing worse than thinking the boss's mom was hot would be the boss's mom knowing he did.

Actually, *the boss* knowing it would probably be worse. Since he was here to fill out paperwork and technically his first day wasn't until tomorrow, it wouldn't be a good idea to piss off Lane before he'd even started. Then there was the fact Lane was strong and knew his way around chain saws. And also owned a commercial wood chipper. Not that

Riley was a slouch in the strength and chain-saw department, but they'd probably be even odds in a fight.

He didn't want to get in a brawl. He also didn't want to lose the job he hadn't even started yet.

"All done," he said in a voice that was rougher than he'd intended. Luckily, she didn't seem to notice as she spun her chair back to face him.

When he handed the clipboard back to her—minus the paper with the guys' contact numbers listed—he was careful to extend his arm fully, rather than lean in again. Then he tried to find something—anything—to stare at rather than the way she ran the end of her pen back and forth across her bottom lip.

She frowned and tapped the lucky pen on the paper, in the area where he'd filled in his current address. "That's a bit of a commute."

"About forty minutes," he said. "It's a hike, but it's doable. Lane said I can leave my gear in the shop, so I can ride my bike, which takes some of the sting out of the drive. After a couple of weeks, if everything's working out for everybody, I'll probably start looking for a place around here."

She frowned. "You're going to ride a bike back and forth?"

"Oh, a motorcycle kind of bike, not a ten-speed. My Harley." She laughed—a low, self-deprecating chuckle—and he wanted to hear more of it. "I'm not sure how far I'd get down the road before somebody called the police to report a man with a chain saw in his bike's basket."

That was better. A real laugh that filled the room and made her eyes crinkle. There was nothing sexier to Riley than a smart woman with a great sense of humor, and he got the impression Laura laughed a lot.

When he'd seen the ad for the job, he'd given it a lot of thought. It was a big change, and he'd have to leave the tree service he'd been with for years. And despite the way he'd shrugged it off for Laura, the commute would be too much—especially in the winter—and he'd have to move. He was used to being close enough to his family to stop by for still-warm cookies or to fix a leaky faucet. But he'd also been unhappy with the stagnation at his current job. He wanted more authority, and more variation in his workdays.

The back-and-forth of the pros-and-cons list had felt endless. But one thing he hadn't even considered was that he might find the new boss's mother incredibly attractive.

He was in so much trouble.

It had been a long time since a man being in the room made Laura wonder if her hair looked okay. And it didn't stop there. There was something about the way Riley McLaughlin looked at her that made her remember that, while a woman was absolutely capable of taking care of her own needs, it was *really* nice to feel the touch of a man's hands sometimes.

And remembering *that* made her feel itchy for things she didn't have the time or energy for, so she tried to focus on the words written on the paperwork in front of her.

Like his date of birth.

He was thirty-nine years old, and she wouldn't have guessed that. He looked younger. He was only eight years older than her son, for goodness' sake. And sure, he was only nine years younger than she was. People probably wouldn't even notice the difference if they were alone. But she had no doubt if the three of them went somewhere, everybody would assume she was *the mom*.

Her gaze skipped down the page to the space at the bottom.

Emergency contact: Kristine McLaughlin.

Relationship: Mother.

And a phone number.

Maybe there was another reason for a wife or girl-friend not to be listed, but the most obvious one was that he was single. She couldn't see how, though. He was thirty-nine, he earned good money and his looks would turn any woman's head.

He was probably taller than average, though not noticeably so. But he had broad shoulders, and his T-shirt showed off the muscles in his chest and arms from a lifetime of hard work. His hair was a dark blond, cut short, and his eyes were a murky blue-green-gray combination that reminded her of the ocean on a cloudy day.

But looks weren't everything, so maybe he was a jerk. She'd just met the guy, and he'd be putting his most charming self forward for a new job. Maybe he was single because he *wasn't* a great guy. Or he could be divorced.

Not that it mattered to her, of course. Even if she wanted a man in her life—and she definitely didn't—it wouldn't be a younger man who worked for her son.

"How do you feel about funeral homes?" she asked suddenly, because no good would come from her current train of thought.

It wasn't until he almost choked on his water that she realized she'd asked that admittedly odd question rather abruptly. "I try to avoid them, for the most part."

She laughed, shaking her head. "I probably should have given you some context *before* I asked."

"I wasn't sure if it was a pop psychology quiz. You can't be too careful around guys with chain saws, I guess."

"Just so you know, when Lane was a teenager, he thought it would be funny to put on a hockey mask and start his chain saw outside my office window."

He chuckled. "Good prank."

"He got four stitches and had to pay to replace the window, so he might disagree."

"What did you throw?"

"My big stapler."

The admiration and amusement in the way he looked at her made her blush. "Noted. No horror movie pranks."

"Speaking of horror movies, back to the funeral home. The reason I asked is that there's an apartment over the garage that the owners built for their daughter. But Molly's moving in with her fiancé, so it'll be empty. If you're interested, I know Paul and Amanda would hold it for you, but a lot of people get spooked around funeral homes, so that's why I asked."

"I don't know if I'm relieved or disappointed you weren't going to ask me to be your plus-one."

"To a funeral?" She laughed, and then inwardly cringed at the breathy sound. Riley McLaughlin was very good at flirting, and she hadn't thought she was susceptible to that. Apparently, she'd been wrong.

He shrugged, that boyish grin on full display. "Not a typical first date, but sometimes there are snacks and you don't really need to bring flowers."

First date? He was too much, and it was time to circle back to the business at hand. "Let me know if you're interested in the apartment. And I think I've got everything I need here. Do you have any questions for me?"

He looked at her with a wicked glimmer in his eye that made her wonder if he was thinking up all manner of inappropriate questions, and then the corners of his mouth lifted. "I have the office number here, and Lane's, and you put the rest of the guys' numbers, but I don't see a cell phone number for you."

He wanted her number. Laura resisted the urge to fan herself with his completed forms and took the list of numbers from him instead. After writing her name and cell phone number across the bottom, she handed it back.

"Thanks. Lane told me if I need something in the office, to send you a message I'm on my way in, but I can't text the office line."

Of course there was a perfectly reasonable and work-related reason why he'd asked for her number. Her cheeks felt hot, but she smiled. "Well, you can try, but I won't get it. And just so you know, Lane hates texting. He also hates talking on the phone."

"Should I do pantomime?"

"Only if he can see you."

He chuckled. "Any tips for how to communicate with the man outside of text messages or phone calls?"

She waved her hand. "Oh, you can text him. Or call. I just want you to know if he's curt or comes across as grumpy, that's probably why. Case, on the other hand, will talk your ear off either way."

"I'm sure I'll get to know them better. And everybody else with the company, of course."

His voice dropping a little when he said that last part *had* to be her imagination. She was reading things into everything he said, and she needed to stop. "It's a great group of guys. Between the brewery and Becca taking up a lot of Lane's time, you'll probably work most closely with Case going forward, but they're all hard workers."

"I'm looking forward to it." He stood and shifted his paper and the water bottle to his left hand so he could extend his right. "It was a pleasure meeting you, Laura."

She wanted to stand and take a step closer to him

before putting her hand in his, but that would be a bad idea. It was hard enough hiding her reaction to him as it was—assuming she was hiding it at all—so she simply reached up. She could feel the strength in his hand and the calluses from years of hard work, and she inhaled deeply, trying to calm her nerves.

Then his touch was gone and he gave her a warm smile. "I'm sure I'll see you soon."

Laura didn't let herself watch him walk out. She wasn't *that* far gone. But she might have peeked at his reflection in her darkened computer screen until he and his delicious, denim-clad backside were out of sight. Then she sighed and tapped the mouse to wake up the screen.

Time to get back to work.

Usually, calling Ellen would be the first thing she'd do when there was an interesting blip in her day. There was nothing off-limits between her and her best friend, but she didn't reach for her cell phone.

Flirting with the new employee was definitely an interesting blip. But it also wouldn't lead to anything except some very private fantasizing, and if Ellen accidentally mentioned it to one of her daughters and it spread, things would get very awkward.

Nope. Keeping things from Ellen went against her nature, but Laura was going to keep her attraction to Riley McLaughlin all to herself.

Chapter Two

We have an early heads-up for you! Starting August 1, Stonefield Police Department and Stonefield Fire Department will be competing to see who can collect the most back-to-school items in their first annual Badges For Backpacks Drive. They'll supply the backpacks, and you bring the school supplies, healthy snacks (no peanut butter!) and more. You can find lists of desired donations on their websites, as well as ours, and on the websites for the town, library and the school.

—Stonefield Gazette *Facebook Page*

Riley pulled into his parents' driveway and leaned his bike onto the kickstand. After killing the engine, he climbed off and left his helmet on the seat before walking through the open garage into the kitchen.

His mom was in the final stages of preparing dinner, as he'd expected. They were having grilled chicken and pasta salad tonight, from the looks of things. "Hi, Mom."

Kris smiled at her son and stepped out from behind the island to accept his kiss on her cheek. Her long hair, which was the same shades of dark blond as his, was in a ponytail, and she was still wearing the black shirt and tan khakis that were the uniform of the restaurant where she waited tables.

She'd gotten that job when Riley and his sisters were kids, because the morning-to-early-afternoon shift meant she could get them off to school and then be home before they returned. She'd kept the job—according to her—because she got her daily steps in and got to talk to people.

"I don't usually see you this early in the day," she said after a glance at the clock. "Dad's only been home for fifteen minutes."

His dad worked for a bank, so he'd been walking through the door at approximately the same time for most of Riley's life. The end of Riley's workdays tended to vary, but were almost always later than his dad's.

"I don't actually start working until tomorrow. I just went to Stonefield to do paperwork and stuff today." He tried not to think about Laura Thompson, which wasn't easy.

When his mom's smile vanished and she sighed, he knew it was the reminder he was starting a new job. And that the new job would probably end up with him moving, which he suspected was the part she didn't like.

"We're getting older now. I don't like the idea of you being so far away," she said, proving him right.

"It's forty minutes, Mom. Plus, Tammy lives across the street and Tara lives five minutes away, and they both have husbands who can help Dad out if there's something he needs done on a weekday."

"It's not the same," she snapped. Riley managed to keep from rolling his eyes, but he couldn't stop the sigh. "I thought you liked the job you had."

"I did, but I was just one of many in a very big company, and for the last couple years I've been stuck clearing along the power lines and it's boring." The utility companies contracted with tree services to keep the power lines clear of trees and brush, and it was steady work, but it got old fast. "With D&T, I'll be doing all kinds of work, and I'll be in charge. Plus, they're paying me a lot more money."

Her face got a pinched look and she pressed her lips together, which meant she was still unhappy but couldn't think of anything else to say.

Riley dug deep for more patience. He was very well aware his mom loved having all three of her children so close, and that—for her—it wasn't really about control, but about comfort. She didn't like change, and her anxiety usually manifested itself as annoyance or disapproval. Once he'd settled into Stonefield and his new job, and she'd been to visit, she'd feel better about it.

Luckily, Jason—his dad—chose that moment to appear in the kitchen, and the pamphlet in his hand made Kris temporarily forget she was unhappy with her son. Instead, she put her hands on her hips and glared at her husband.

"Riley, tell your father I'm not going on a cruise with him."

"I feel like that's the kind of thing *you* could tell him."

"I have—three times—and he doesn't seem to believe me."

His dad held up the pamphlet. "Riley, tell your mother how fun cruises are."

"One, I've never been on a cruise, so I have no idea if they're fun or not. And two—*again*—that feels like something you could tell her yourself."

"I have, but she doesn't seem to believe me."

Riley chuckled and left them to their game. The bickering was good-natured and baked into their relationship, along with love, laughter and an occasional conflict flare-up. He knew at some point in the future, they'd be going on a cruise. It would just take his dad a while to get past his mom's anxiety about doing something new and spending that much money.

"While you're here, son, I could use a hand in the garage," his dad said, nodding toward the door.

On his way past, Jason set the cruise brochure on the kitchen island. Kris sniffed and then turned her back on it.

Once they were in the garage, his dad took a couple of sodas out of the overflow fridge and handed one to Riley. "So how did the meeting go?"

"Good." His mom must have been venting a lot for his dad to know this was a garage conversation. "It's a good setup, the guys seem decent, and the equipment isn't new, but it's well maintained."

And then there is the boss's mom, though Riley had no intention of telling his dad he got a little hot and bothered every time he thought about Laura Thompson. His dad would expend a lot of energy giving him a lecture on the many reasons pursuing that attraction was a very bad idea, and he didn't need to. Riley already knew them.

"Hell of a commute, though."

"Only for a couple of weeks, or a month, tops. Once I'm sure it's a good fit for me, I'll look for a place in Stonefield and let my apartment go."

As was his way, Jason McLaughlin didn't express how he felt about his only son moving farther away from home. He always went straight to practicalities. "What's the real estate market like there? Maybe it's time to buy instead of continuing to rent."

He'd gotten the lecture about buying a house being an investment while renting was setting money on fire when he'd moved into his current apartment.

And he'd gotten it for each of the two apartments before that.

"I might rent a place short-term," he said, and remembering the funeral home discussion with Laura made him smile. "I want to get to know the town a little before I invest in the real estate."

His dad frowned for a moment before nodding. "I guess that makes sense. Are you staying for dinner?"

Riley shook his head. "I'm going to grab something on the way home and call it a night early. Getting up forty minutes earlier in the morning's going to kick my butt for a few days."

"I hope it works out for you. I know it's a big move."

"Yeah. It's the right one, though." He shrugged. "I think. I *hope*."

Working for a family-run business added layers to the company dynamic that could be hard for an outsider to navigate. Even the smallest of conflicts with a coworker could suddenly be a big conflict with all of the powers that be, thanks to the loyalty of family ties.

And that was why later, when he was going through the process of adding the printed list of D&T Tree Service contacts to his phone, Laura's number made him hesitate. He was tempted to enter her as *Lane's mom* so it would act as a constant reminder she was off-limits. But the memory of her annoyance with her son for introducing her to him that way stopped him.

He was going to have to rely on willpower and

common sense to keep him in check. Laura Thompson was definitely off-limits.

Laura heard the rumble of a Harley engine in the distance, and she didn't bother feeling guilty about the thrill of anticipation that accompanied the sound.

As long as nobody knew she was having very inappropriate thoughts about an employee, who cared? And Lane and Case owned the company. She got paid by them the same as Riley did. They were coworkers. He was still too young for her, though, which was why she wasn't going to share those inappropriate thoughts with anybody.

Because the guys usually showed up and started their day before customers started calling, Laura liked to sit on her front porch and drink a second cup of coffee on nice mornings. Not all the time, but often enough she could lie to herself about not being on the porch to get a glimpse of Riley as he arrived.

The way her pulse quickened when he came into sight wasn't a lie, though. The dark gray D&T Tree Service shirt he'd been given yesterday stretched tight over his chest and biceps and was tucked into jeans that hugged his thighs. The relaxed way he sat on the bike, with his legs extended so his boots rested on the pegs, invited her gaze to explore the length of his body.

And it did. Laura sipped her coffee slowly, watching him over the rim of her mug, as the bike slowed so he could turn into the lower driveway. It definitely wasn't a bad way to start the day.

As she watched, Lane stepped out of the garage and waved Riley over to a spot under the protection of the pole barn that he'd cleaned out for the new guy's Harley. She savored the view of Riley's muscles flexing as he stood and swung his leg over the bike before taking his helmet off.

But when they started talking, Laura sighed and turned her attention back to the birds fluttering around her flowers. It wasn't nearly as fun to lust after the man while he was talking to her son.

Ten minutes later, they all rolled out, and she caught a glimpse of Riley riding shotgun in the big boom truck. As they drove past the house, she thought he leaned forward so he could see the porch. And he might have smiled at her.

Or it could have been her imagination, she thought as she stood and went back inside. Ridiculous wishful thinking. The man might be a flirt, but that was it. He was ingratiating himself with his new boss's mom—who was also the office staff—and she had a fresh fantasy to amuse herself with. Nothing more.

She hadn't even been settled at her desk for fifteen minutes before Evie walked in with the baby. Laura had heard them in the kitchen when she came in, so she'd detoured straight to her office. She tried to give them their space as much as possible, and she hadn't wanted to interrupt them. But she was always happy to have them interrupt *her*, and she was smiling when she spun her chair to face them.

"Did the guys already leave?" Evie asked as she crossed the room with the baby.

"They pulled out a few minutes ago." She put out her hands and felt the familiar rush of pleasure when Becca reached for her. "Hey, baby girl."

"I wanted to meet the new guy," Evie said, plopping onto the armchair. "Riley…something, right?"

"Riley McLaughlin." She ignored the flutter in her belly thinking about him triggered.

"Lane said he's going to be a good fit. What did you think of him?"

Making a sex joke about how she also thought he'd be a good fit—in a totally different way—was out of the question. "I think he'll work out."

"Okay, but what about on a personal level? Is he nice? Funny? Does he actually use words instead of grunting like Bruce?"

Laura laughed. Bruce Fletcher was one of their best workers, but people made him uncomfortable and he wasn't exactly a great conversationalist. "Riley uses words. And he's pretty funny. Charming. A little bit of a flirt."

When Evie's eyebrows shot up, Laura realized she should have left that last bit out. "He flirted with you?"

"Of course not," Laura fibbed, keeping her eyes on Becca's adorable face so Evie couldn't see them. "I just meant you can tell he's the type."

When Evie made a noncommittal sound, Laura looked up. Her daughter-in-law didn't believe her. But Becca chose that moment to let out an impressive burp, so she was saved from that conversation when Evie sighed and threw up her hands.

"I swear that girl burps more than her father does. And she's louder, too."

Laura booped her granddaughter's nose with the tip of her finger. "That's why she's such a happy baby, right, Becca?"

"Speaking of Becca being such a happy baby, can you watch her for a little while? Gwen's publisher wants her to film some short videos to promote the new book and you know how she is."

Laura did know how she was. Gwen Danforth, who still wrote as Gwen Sutton, hated promoting her books—or herself—but she'd gotten better at it once Evie moved back to town. Evie loved social media, and she not only handled the accounts for Sutton's Place Brewery & Tavern, but she'd taken over the tree service's Facebook Page. And whenever her publicist needed content from Gwen, Evie got roped in.

"Of course I'll watch her. My goal is for her to be able to run this office by the time she's five or six so I can retire."

Evie laughed. "Make sure you teach her how to negotiate for raises."

"Of course. And Ellen said Jack's still determined to work for his uncles and eventually take over the tree service, so I think it'll be a family business for a long time."

Mallory was the middle Sutton sister, and her older son had been talking about working with Case and Lane for years. Laura knew it wouldn't be long before they had the kid out in the woods, dragging brush for the crew to run through the chipper.

"I shouldn't be more than a couple of hours," Evie said. "Probably less, since Gwen hates doing videos."

"Take your time. You know we'll be fine."

Evie leaned down to kiss the top of Becca's head. "Be good for Nana, okay?"

Becca burped and Laura was still laughing when the front door closed behind Evie. She put the baby in the playpen that occupied the corner of her office, adding Becca's favorite toys.

Then, since Becca would get bored after a while and demand Nana's attention, Laura woke up her computer and forced herself to get some work done. Work that included adding their new hire to the payroll system, which put Riley smack-dab in the center of her thoughts again.

Lane and Case had talked about what an incredible stroke of luck it was that Riley McLaughlin was looking to make a change, just when they'd decided they wanted to hire somebody who could run the crew so they could take a little step back. They'd crossed paths with him over the years and they liked him. And he was definitely qualified. There wasn't a single box he didn't check, and within two minutes of Laura forwarding his application email to Lane, he'd called to tell her to pull the ad and notify other applicants that the position had been filled. The interview at the taproom had been a formality with the bonus of good beer.

She couldn't mess this up for them.

Riley might be a flirt, but there was almost no chance a man who looked like that would be interested in a woman her age. Riley feeling awkward—or even, heaven forbid, uncomfortable—would definitely mess with the workplace dynamics.

If that happened and any of the other guys caught on, she'd end up being the subject of gossip all over town—Lane Thompson's mom lusting after his new employee. And she didn't even want to think about the cougar jokes.

She'd keep her mind out of the gutter and her eyes off his butt, and eventually the infatuation would fade. It had to.

Chapter Three

*A question was raised after a heated debate in
the middle of Main Street earlier this week, so
we reached out to the police department for a
definite answer from the chief: "Yes, you do
have to stop for pedestrians even if they're not in
a [redacted] crosswalk because you [redacted]
can't just [redacted] run people over." I think
we'll be holding further questions for Chief
Bordeaux until the heat breaks.*

—Stonefield Gazette *Facebook Page*

"I thought maybe you'd go easy on me, this being
my first day and all."

While Lane and Case laughed at him, Riley looked
over the situation. The old pine was very tall, half-

way to being dead and right between two very expensive lakefront cottages. The tree couldn't go in the water and it certainly couldn't land on either of the cottages, so it had to be dropped uphill into a very narrow opening, and preferably not into the professionally landscaped gardens behind the larger of the two cottages.

"Okay," he said once he'd gone through it a couple of times in his mind.

He looked at Lane and Case, but they just waited, arms folded across their chests. Riley knew he was being tested, so he walked them through how they'd limb it, take the top first and then cut off lengths. It was going to be a hell of a lot of work, even with the two young guys—Neil and Shane—they'd brought along to do the dragging and cleanup. And to hold the ropes that would keep limbs from swinging into buildings, of course.

When he was done talking, Lane nodded and then Case clapped his hands together. "Well, let's get it done."

Riley noticed both Neil and Shane put their cell phones in the cab of Case's truck before getting to work, and he moved toward it to do the same as he pulled his phone out of his pocket. Lane stopped him with a quick head shake.

"You keep yours in case of an emergency," he said. "Unless you're going to hang around up there texting your girlfriend."

"Nope. Don't have a girlfriend, and I prefer to pay

attention when chain-saw blades and tree limbs are in motion."

Riley was afraid he'd find out Case and Lane had been working together so long, they'd have a rhythm and way of doing things that he'd have a hard time catching on to. But the three of them worked well together. His new bosses were big on safety and communication, and he could tell within the first few minutes that they knew what they were doing. And he learned over the course of the day that they were damn good at it.

By the time he'd finished the last undercut, taking a V-shaped notch out of the base of the tree to determine the direction it would fall, his shoulders and back ached. He'd been clearing power lines for so long, he'd forgotten how the stress of needing a clean drop could settle into tension in the muscles. And he was working those muscles a little harder than usual.

But as he moved around to the other side of the tree to make the back cut, he knew he'd made the right decision in coming to D&T. He'd wanted a challenge and they'd given him one. Finishing the horizontal cut slightly above the notch cut out of the other side, making a hinge effect, he took a step back and watched the remains of the trunk fall exactly where he wanted them to.

With the hard part of the job done, Riley decided it was time for a break. He leaned against the boom truck, since it was big enough to offer a decent amount of shade. He wasn't surprised when Boomer appeared next to his boot. The dog liked to nap under the truck, apparently. Case had found the German shepherd and black Lab mix there one day—hence the name Boomer—and when nobody had claimed him, Case kept him.

Riley loved dogs, especially the kind that could go to work with you and happily hang out in the shade all day. He'd never had one of his own, since leaving a dog home during all the hours he worked didn't seem fair, and his former employer didn't allow dogs on the job. But maybe once his position in the company was solid, and if he could find a rescue as awesome as Boomer, he'd think about it.

"You thirsty, bud?" he asked the dog, and when his ears alerted, Riley walked to Case's truck. There was a bowl on the ground by the back tire, and he refilled it from a jug Case kept on the floor of the back seat.

"Did I pass the test?" he asked when Case joined him.

The other man chuckled. "I told Lane we're not as subtle as we think we are. And hell yes, you passed. We knew you would. But what about us? Did *we* pass?"

"Hell yes." He nodded, and when Boomer sat in front of him, he reached down and scratched behind his ears. "I like the way you work. And also, there's this good boy here."

"I was surprised he came today. Since Gwen

moved in, he's gotten a little spoiled, and when it's hot like this, he usually stays home with her. It used to be that he only played hooky during January and February, when it's bitter cold."

Riley chuckled and gave the dog a final scratch before straightening. His back muscles protested, and he knew he'd be running the shower hot and hard tonight. "When we met for the interview, Lane said your dads started the company and you two are cousins, but you have different last names. So not brothers or…"

"My dad was Aunt Laura's brother, so they were brothers-in-law. I guess my dad and Uncle Joe didn't like each other at first, but over time they became friends and they both wanted to work for themselves. It was basically two guys with chain saws for a while, but they worked hard and built it into something."

Riley was still stuck on *Aunt Laura*. Another thing he'd known on a logical level, but hadn't really given much thought to. She wasn't only his new boss's mom. She was his other new boss's aunt.

"Lane stepped in when Uncle Joe died about… I don't know. Twelve years ago, now? I worked with them, and when my dad passed away five years ago, his half became mine. My mom was already gone, two years before my dad, but we had Aunt Laura to keep us on track while we learned how to run it together." He paused to chuckle. "We still have her keeping us on track."

Riley was spared from having to respond to that

when Lane approached and slapped him on the shoulder. "Damn good work. Case was smart to listen to me when I said we should hire you."

"Yes, *you* were smart to listen to *me*," Case retorted, and they all laughed.

"So what now?" Riley asked, ready to get back to it before his muscles started stiffening up on him.

"We're done here for the day," Case told him. "Bruce usually does our ongoing contracts for power lines and some rec trails, but he'll bring Neil and Shane back tomorrow to clean up and deal with the stump. You can go out with Bruce's crew tomorrow so you get a chance to know those guys. And we've got two brothers—Zeb and Jonah—who do property-maintenance-type stuff. Trimming small trees and taking care of shrubs and whatnot. It crosses over into landscaping a little, but we like to have a lot of irons in the fire."

By the time they got back to the pit, as they called the equipment area around the garage, Riley was wishing he'd driven his truck in that morning. He loved the bike, but in his truck he could blast the air-conditioning while using the heated lumbar support in his seat to soothe his back.

Case and the younger guys took off right away, but Lane gestured for Riley to follow him into the garage. They erased the day's job from one of two large, color-coded whiteboards that showed where most of the guys would be for each day that week.

"Only the three of us touch this board," Lane said.

"That board's for Bruce's crew—just for the big utility company contracts. He handles that board and nobody but him touches it. Although, to be honest, I'm not sure when the last time he checked it is. They know what they're doing pretty much months in advance, and he's got his own system. This just makes my mom happy."

"Got it."

"All that's left is customer payment, I guess. We've had some tech issues—and user errors—so if somebody wants to pay with a card, they can either call Mom or there's a web address at the bottom of the paperwork with a secure payment link. Most of our customers pay with cash or a check, and you should bring that up to Mom at the end of the day."

Riley winced. While he didn't call his own parents by their first names, he kind of wished Lane was one of those adult children who did. Hearing his boss call her Laura instead of Mom would make him feel slightly less guilty about how much time he'd spent thinking about her last night—especially since he'd been thinking about having his mouth and his hands on her.

"We used to have a box in here," Lane was saying, "but then a guy we'd just hired decided he'd take it home with him."

"Ouch."

"Yeah. Luckily, he also thought it would be a good idea to take the checks to the bank here in town and ask Rene to cash them for him, as if she hasn't been handling the tree service since the business opened."

"I'm guessing that was the last day he worked for you."

"Absolutely." Lane snorted. "None of us were going to trust him to be smart enough to wield a chain saw around us after that. Also, he did a little time for that one."

Riley chuckled and then took the checks Lane handed to him. "You want me to take these up to the house?"

"I figure you may as well get the feel for everything. Plus, I have to look at the axle on that chipper, and you taking them means I don't have to walk over there and back."

"It's good to be the boss," Riley said, and they were both laughing when he walked out of the garage. He was halfway to the house when he remembered he was supposed to text first, though, so he pulled out his phone and typed while he walked.

It's Riley. I've got some checks for you.

He was almost to the porch when the reply came through.

I like checks. Come on in.

As he climbed the steps, he reminded himself for the umpteenth time that, yes, he was extremely attracted to Laura Thompson, but, no, he couldn't allow himself to act on it. That wouldn't be easy.

And he'd been thinking about her all day, so even though he'd have to keep his hands and his inappropriate thoughts to himself, he wasn't sure he'd be able to hide how happy he was to see her again so soon.

It took Laura a few seconds to realize the high-pitched squealing sound had come from her and not Becca. The baby was happily banging two toys together in her playpen, though she paused now and looked at her grandmother.

Just seeing Riley's name on her screen had been enough to make her squeal and hug her phone to her chest like a teenager. She forced herself to take a deep, calming breath and told herself to be thankful the only other person in the room was six months old.

By the time she heard the footsteps approaching her office, she was pretty sure she had her face under control. There was nothing she could do about her heart rate, though. Her pulse had quickened the second she'd realized she was going to see him again, and it didn't seem inclined to resume its usual rhythm.

Suddenly, she had no idea what to do with herself. She was too jumpy to pull off sitting casually at the desk, and she didn't want him to guess she was having any kind of reaction to being alone with him again.

Almost alone.

She crossed the room and lifted Becca out of her

playpen. Holding the baby grounded her, reminding her she was a forty-eight-year-old grandmother and not a teenager in the first throes of infatuation.

It worked, right up until Riley stepped into her office and she looked into his sea-colored eyes.

"Hey, Laura," he said in a low voice that would sound perfect in the dark, with their heads sharing a pillow. Then his gaze shifted to the baby on her hip. "And who's this little beauty?"

"This is Becca." She hesitated for a second. "My granddaughter."

That would be a fire hose dousing any heat sizzling between them.

But he stepped closer so he could see Becca better, and that put him close enough to Laura that she could inhale the scent of him. Sweat. The burnt-oil smell of two-stroke exhaust. He needed a shower, but she didn't mind. She was used to the smell of hard work.

"You have your grandma's pretty eyes, Becca," he said, and the baby wiggled, reaching for him.

"I'm Nana," Laura said, surprised when he put his hands under Becca's reaching arms and easily lifted her. He was clearly comfortable with babies, and Becca had no anxiety around strangers, which was both good and bad. "Ellen—Evie's mom and my best friend—was already Grammy to Mallory's boys, so I'm Nana to make things less confusing for everybody, but especially for Becca."

He bounced Becca gently, and she laughed in delight. "So you have *Nana's* pretty eyes, and her pretty smile, too."

Riley looked at Laura over the baby's head as he said the words, and her cheeks grew warm. None of the heat had been doused. He was actually still flirting with a woman he'd just referred to as *Nana*.

And Becca had Lane's eyes and smile, of course, along with Evie's nose and blond hair—for now, though it would probably darken over time—but Laura wasn't going to argue with him. She'd tuck the compliment away to savor later.

"I wish she'd stop going to every stranger who wants to pick her up," she said, because talking about the baby was safest. "I mean, not that she should be suspicious of *you*, specifically, but…you know what I mean."

"I do. And if it makes you feel any better, babies love me. I have five nieces and nephews, so I've had plenty of practice keeping them happy."

"Five? Wow. Any of your own?" she asked, trying to sound as casual as possible. He hadn't listed any kids on his forms, including the insurance, but sometimes they were on the mother's policy.

"Nope. My sisters' kids keep me plenty busy, especially when it's Christmas shopping time."

She had so many other questions she wanted to ask. Had he ever been married? And did he *want* kids? Was he looking for a young woman who'd give him a family?

But she couldn't bring herself to ask questions

so personal—or revealing—so she went back to a conversational safe ground. "So do you have one sister with five kids, or multiple sisters who each have kids?"

He grinned, making her heart skip. "Two sisters, both younger. I'm the big brother. Tammy has two girls and one boy, and Tara has one of each. They range from eight down to eighteen months. They both live less than five minutes from our parents. I was the black sheep and moved ten minutes from them."

Laura laughed, which made Becca laugh and wiggle in Riley's arms. "Moving to Stonefield would really be a rogue move."

"So I've been told," he said in a light tone. "I have those checks in my back pocket, but this cutie's a squirmy one."

For one confusing moment, Laura thought he was suggesting she reach into his pocket for the checks. Then she realized he meant she should take Becca and gave a breathy laugh.

"Come on back to Nana, sweetheart."

Of course the baby didn't want to leave the interesting new person with the slightly scratchy jaw who smelled like Daddy to go back to boring old Nana. She grabbed his T-shirt in both little fists and refused to let go.

They were already in the act of transferring her, so Laura had to close the small gap between her body and Riley's to keep Becca from dangling while they disentangled her tiny fingers from his shirt. His chest was a hard wall against her upper arm and warmth flooded through her.

"I've got her, if you want to try to get your shirt back," Laura told him, hoping he wouldn't notice the quiver in her voice.

"She's got quite a grip."

Riley's head was close to hers, and she focused on trying to control her breathing. And the baby. Right now Becca was the only thing keeping her from turning fully to him and possibly making a fool of herself, therefore making working with him that much more awkward.

Then his hands, which were covering Becca's as he tried to tempt her to let go of his shirt and grab his fingers, stilled. There was hardly any space now between the side of her body and the front of his, and he leaned in, inhaling deeply. He wasn't quite touching her neck, but when he let out the breath, it was like a soft touch trailing over her skin.

Her own breath caught in her chest, and she closed her eyes for a moment, imagining the kiss that would come next if she wasn't holding the baby. The baby who picked that second to let go of Riley's shirt and grab hers instead. Freed from Becca, Riley's hand skimmed lightly over Laura's back.

The front door closed and they moved at the same time. With distance between them, Laura kept her attention on Becca. She heard Riley clear his throat harshly, but she didn't look at him. She was afraid he'd see the desire for him written all over her face. And it also gave her a few seconds to compose herself before Lane walked in.

"Hey, Mom. Oh, and there's my best girl!"

Becca started wiggling and kicking as soon as she saw her daddy, so Laura handed her off to Lane. Holding her had given her something to do and somebody to look at, so now she had nothing grounding her.

She turned to Riley, since he was holding the checks out to her, and their gazes met. Thankfully, her son's focus was all on his daughter, because there was no disguising the hunger in the look Riley was giving her.

He wasn't just flirting out of habit, or trying to charm the office staff at his new job. Riley wanted her and he was doing a poor job of hiding it. And she was afraid she wasn't any better at it.

After taking the checks, she had an excuse to go to her desk. Sitting allowed her to hide her face from both men, and she took a long drink from the water tumbler she kept next to her calculator.

"Tomorrow will be an easy day for you, since you're riding with Bruce's crew," Lane told Riley. "Starting next week, you'll essentially take over my place in the company, working with Case, and I'll float around where I'm needed."

"Sounds good. If I had a little one like this little cutie at home, I'd cut back on my hours, too. I guess I'll head out now. I'll see you later, Laura."

It sounded like a promise, and Laura didn't trust herself to turn around. "Good night, Riley."

Lane took Becca with him, and she could hear him talking to Riley as the men left the office.

"Case took up so much of the slack while we were trying to get the brewery up and running. Now that it's more successful than any of us dreamed, Irish has been taking up the slack there. Trying to do both while becoming a dad has been too much for me and too much to ask of them, so we're all glad you're here."

They were too far away for Laura to hear how Riley responded, and she let her head fall to the desk. The wood was cool against her warm forehead, and she made a low growling sound of frustration.

This wasn't an itch she wouldn't mind having scratched. It was a full-blown *ache* now, and she was doomed.

Chapter Four

We might be having a heat wave, but Sutton's Seconds is already thinking snow! It's a perfect time to stay in the air-conditioning and do some decluttering. Bring gently-used items and clothing to the thrift store and they'll make you an offer. They're already seeking clothing and outerwear for the cooler days that are coming soon (we hope)!

—Stonefield Gazette *Facebook Page*

The only thing worse than moving was moving during some of the hottest days of the summer.

By the end of his third day of work, Riley had known two things. One, he was going to be happy working for D&T Tree Service for the long term.

And two, the commute was too much. After a full day of hard work in the heat and humidity, the cooling off—whether from the truck's AC or the wind if he was on the bike—made him sleepy.

He'd sent a text message to Laura, asking if the funeral home apartment was still available, and he'd been hoping getting the information would give him an excuse to see her. He hadn't had a reason to go in the house since dropping off the checks. But fifteen minutes later, she'd sent him a response. The apartment was available, Amanda said he could have it and he could move in immediately. The monthly rent figure she included was more than fair, maybe because it was a funeral home. There had also been an address and phone number, so all he could do was thank her. No reason to go into the office.

He'd stopped at the funeral home after work that day. He met Paul and Amanda Cyrs, who seemed nice. He also met his neighbors on the other side. Callan, who was the librarian in town, and Molly—his fiancée and the Cyrses' daughter. She'd lived in the apartment until she moved next door. The apartment was small, but open and cheerful. He gave them money the next day and they gave him the key.

"Living at a funeral home is weird." The voice of Colby, his oldest friend from childhood, broke into Riley's thoughts.

Seth, a friend he'd worked with for years, nodded. "It's creepy, dude."

"I live over the garage."

"The *hearse* garage," Seth pointed out.

When he'd asked his two closest friends to give up an entire weekend during the height of summer to help him move, Riley had deliberately not mentioned the funeral home aspect of his new address. Instead, he'd let it be a surprise, and they had a lot of opinions about it.

"Let's bring those last boxes up and we'll be done," he said, hoping to distract them with the promise of pizza and beer. It was a small price to pay for getting the whole move done during his two days off.

He owed both his sisters babysitting time, which was a harder debt to pay off. His mom had watched the littlest ones while the older kids were at school. Tammy was an at-home mom, but Tara had burned a sick day, and they'd packed pretty much everything he owned while he was at work. The guys had still carried a lot of loose items, and his clothes had made the trip in garbage bags, but it was done.

Of course, unpacking was going to take a while, but at least he didn't have to worry about falling asleep on his way home from work anymore. Paul had given him a corner of the garage for his Harley, and he could park his truck in the driveway unless there was a funeral function going on. He'd given Amanda his spare key to keep in her office in case he was out on his bike and they needed to move it.

Colby and Seth would be heading home after eating, so they showed up at Sutton's Place Brewery & Tavern in three separate trucks. Luckily, they weren't too busy on a Sunday, late afternoon, so he didn't feel bad about taking up the parking.

He heard her laugh as soon as he stepped through the door.

Laura was here, and he couldn't stop himself from scanning the room until he spotted her. She was sitting at a table toward the back with a group of women, and they were all laughing. It was her laughter that caught his attention, though, and if Colby hadn't nudged him and nodded his head toward an empty table nearby, he might not have been able to stop himself from walking straight to her.

Instead, he followed Colby and Seth to the table. Because they sat first, he was left with the empty chair. It faced Laura's direction, and he was tempted to make one of his friends move. But they'd only ask questions he didn't want to answer, so he sat and tried not to look at her.

After a short discussion about toppings, Riley called the Stonefield House of Pizza for two large pizzas to be delivered to the taproom. On the ride to a job earlier in the week, one of the guys had filled him in on food at the taproom. They had the popcorn machine, and they did some appetizer-type foods. Mozzarella sticks and nachos and such. But they didn't have a full restaurant kitchen, so they had an arrangement with the pizza place for deliveries.

Molly Cyrs, his landlords' daughter, approached their table with her long, dark ponytail swinging and a smile on her face. "Hi, guys!"

"I didn't realize you work here," he said.

"I don't." He must have looked confused, because she laughed. "Not officially. Once a job is official, it's a lot less fun, so I just help out."

"Okay." Whatever made her happy. "What's good on tap tonight?"

"Everything," she said quickly, but then she gave them a rundown on the brews currently available, all of which were brewed in the cellar under them by Lane and Irish—the cowboy in hat and boots behind the bar.

Once they had their beer, Riley took a long swallow and tried not to think about the woman at the other end of the room. He tried not to remember the way he'd felt when their bodies were almost pressed together and he'd lowered his face *almost* to her neck, wanting nothing more than to press his mouth to her skin.

If she hadn't been holding the baby... Nope. He wasn't thinking about that right now.

Then she laughed again, and there wasn't a force in the universe that could have stopped him from looking.

And this time she caught him. Their eyes met, and even from a distance, he could see she had the same reaction when she saw him that he did when he saw her. That catch of the breath. A slight flush over the skin. Lips parting slightly.

But he also saw the woman next to her register that she'd lost Laura's attention and follow her gaze straight to Riley. The woman looked at him for a few seconds and then said something to Laura.

She looked guilty as hell, he thought, when she startled and turned back to her friend. She said something, and then the other woman waved to him, gesturing him over to their table.

Oh, damn. There was no way out of it, so he interrupted Colby and Seth's debate on which of their beers was better and told them he'd be right back. Then he pushed his chair back and stood, praying his life wasn't about to get a whole lot more complicated.

Laura knew if she'd ever gotten the acting bug and headed to Hollywood, she would have been lucky to land a toilet cleanser commercial, and she certainly never would have walked the red carpet to get an award. She had zero acting skills.

But she still tried to look nonchalant as Riley walked across the taproom. When Ellen had noticed her looking at him and asked who he was, she'd told her he was the new guy at the tree service and that should have been enough. But, of course, Ellen had to wave him over.

"I hear you're the new guy," Ellen said when he reached their table.

He laughed and nodded. "That's me. The new guy."

"This is Riley," Laura said, waving her hand at him. "Riley, this is Ellen Sutton, a very dear friend of mine."

"Ah, your co-grandmother."

"Yes," Ellen said, obviously pleased. "And this is my daughter Gwen. She's Case's wife and obviously you know him. And this is my daughter Mallory. That little bundle of cuteness tucked in the sling is Leeza, my new grandbaby. Leeza's daddy is Irish Sutton, of course. The cowboy behind the bar."

Riley's eyes were wide when he smiled, and Laura imagined he was trying to track all the family relationships in his mind. It was a lot to throw at him, and she laughed. "I should hang a big family tree in the office."

"Or a spreadsheet," Gwen said. "But it's nice to meet you, Riley. There won't be a quiz after, so take all the time you need figuring out who everybody is."

"Wait. Irish's last name is Sutton?"

Gwen nodded. "When he moved to town, he only went by Irish, which was his last name. There were personal reasons he didn't use his given name. When he and Mallory got married, he took the Sutton name."

"Got it."

"You've met Evie, right?" Ellen asked. "The third of my girls."

"I met her outside the garage one day," he said, and Laura could see he was starting to get anxious and wanted to return to his friends. And he was very pointedly not looking at her.

"Amanda told me you were moving in this weekend," Ellen said. "If you find yourself needing anything, Sutton's Seconds is my thrift store, and we have a little bit of everything."

"Voted Best Thrift Store in New Hampshire two years in a row," Gwen and Mallory said together, and they all laughed.

"I'll be sure to stop in," Riley said, and then he looked around the table, his gaze catching on Laura just long enough to make her nerves dance. "I should get back to my friends, but it was lovely to meet you all. Have a good night, ladies."

None of them were shy about watching him walk away, and Laura certainly understood it, but she didn't like it.

"He's a handsome one," Gwen said when he was out of earshot. "It's too bad he's too young for you, Laura."

Her gaze jerked to Gwen's, and she was afraid she'd given herself away. But then she remembered Evie telling her that she, Gwen and Mal thought Laura was way overdue for having a good time, which meant her lack of a dating life was an ongoing conversation between the sisters.

"He's not as young as he looks," Laura said, instantly regretting it. Arguing against not being able to date Riley might make it look as if she'd given it some thought. "But yes. He's too young for me."

"He's around Lane's age, right?" Gwen asked.

"He's thirty-nine, actually."

"But he works for Lane and Case," Mallory added. "That would be awkward."

"There's gotta be somebody in this town you could date, Laura," Gwen said, reaching forward to dredge a tortilla chip through congealing nacho cheese.

"I have zero interest in dating," Laura said emphatically. Other than this inexplicable crush she seemed to have on Riley, it was the truth.

She'd gone out with a few guys after Joe died—mostly friends of David Sutton. Double-dating with Ellen and her husband had been a low-key way to get back out there. But eventually the men would start talking about the future and Laura would lose interest very quickly. While it was nice to have the company of a man sometimes, she was never giving up control of her life again.

At some point, it had become easier to see to her own needs—she had a gadget in the kitchen to open jars and a gadget in her nightstand drawer for orgasms—and not bother with men at all.

Meeting Riley had shaken her up a little, though. Clearly she was *not* through with men, though it would have been nice if the reaction hadn't been triggered by somebody she had to deny herself.

"She doesn't need to date anybody," Ellen told her daughter. "She has me. We're going to be merry widows together and have all kinds of fun adventures."

"I don't think 'merry widow' means what you think it does," Mallory said, and Gwen snorted.

Their mother gave them each a stern look. "I don't care. You know what I mean."

"Lucy and Ethel," Mallory said.

"Lucy and Lucy," Gwen corrected her, and they all laughed again.

When the taproom hosted a costume contest for Halloween, she and Ellen had decided Lucy and Ethel would be the perfect costumes for two best friends. They'd both wanted to be Lucille Ball, though, and neither would give, so they'd both shown up to the party as Lucy.

A mewling sound interrupted them, and they all looked to the fabric sling Mallory was wearing. She smiled down at her daughter, who was only a few weeks old, and the mewling turned into an angry squawk.

"I'll probably head back to the house," Mallory said. "It's cranky time."

"You know you can nurse her here," Gwen said. "Nobody minds, and if somebody did...well, I guess they can take that up with the bartender."

Laura was pretty sure nobody would complain to Irish about his wife feeding his baby in a business he partly owned, but Mallory stood.

"My chair is so much more comfortable," she said. "And I don't even want to talk about the diapers this little one goes through. She's so much more disgusting than her brothers ever were."

Ellen wrinkled her nose, shaking her head. "Jack and Eli were pretty gross."

Since Mallory's boys were ten and twelve now, Laura was sure Mallory had simply forgotten the smellier aspects of their infancy. It was the same for grandmothers, she assumed. When she changed Becca's diaper, she was 100 percent sure it was more disgusting than any of Lane's had been.

"I'm going to go, too," Gwen said, standing. "Case and Boomer were napping, but he's probably up now. I should see if he has any good gossip about the new guy."

Laura made herself smile because everybody else was, but she didn't want to. Everything about this night had reminded her of the many ways Riley was already connected to everybody she knew. She just wanted to fantasize in peace, without worrying she was going to upset every person in her life if she ever had the chance to act some of those fantasies out.

Once Ellen's daughters were gone, she munched another nacho and washed it down with a swallow of soda. "Did you see the next pick for Books & Brews?"

Laura nodded. "I've already started it."

When Callan Avery moved to Stonefield to be the new librarian, he'd brought a lot of ideas to renew interest in the historic library. Books & Brews, a book club that met every second Wednesday at the taproom, was one of the new programs. A book club with booze and nachos was the best kind, and Irish liked having an event bringing in business on their slowest night of the week.

Ellen wrinkled her nose. "It sounds boring."

"It is," Laura said, and they laughed together. "I

don't know why so many book club books have to be gloomy."

"I think Callan's punishing us for letting Molly pick a romance novel last time. Everybody liked it, but the conversation about whether that bit in chapter eight was anatomically possible made him blush so hard he might have permanent capillary damage."

Laura couldn't help it. At the mention of *that bit in chapter eight*, she looked at Riley. He was eating pizza and laughing with his friends, and her heart twisted at the sight of them together.

One of the friends looked about Riley's age and the other a little younger, but together as a group, they looked *young*. Or rather, looking at them made her feel older. If Lane and Case walked in and sat down at Riley's table, they'd fit right in. If she walked over and sat down, people would wonder why she was sitting with them.

Then he caught her eye and smiled, and worries about what other people would think flew out of her mind. After a moment of the kind of eye contact that made her feel like the room was suddenly twenty degrees warmer, she smiled and turned her attention back to Ellen.

"Do you think I should dye my hair?"

Ellen looked startled. "Why?"

"I don't know. I have more gray than you. I feel old."

"It's beautiful the way it is, and if you dye it, you'll have to *keep* dyeing it or the roots will be… You remember Mary two years ago?" Laura winced. "Exactly."

It didn't matter, anyway. Even if she covered the gray, she'd still be forty-eight. And he'd still be too young.

She'd just fill her life with work and Becca and yard sales, book clubs and knitting. If she kept herself busy, she wouldn't spend so much time thinking about what might be missing in her life—what she hadn't missed at all until Riley McLaughlin walked through the door.

Chapter Five

*Due to the number of comments Town Hall has
received about the need to paint the gazebo in
the town square, there will be a special meeting of the budget committee at the library on
Thursday at 3:00 p.m. As always, the public
is invited to attend, but if you've already sub-
mitted a comment on the matter via email or
phone, please note that your opinion has been
counted and you don't need to repeat it. Library
rules regarding food and beverages apply.*
—Stonefield Gazette *Facebook Page*

On Wednesday afternoon, Riley drove back to the
garage with a check burning a hole in his pocket.
Lane had worked half a day because of the brewery,

and Case had left early because Gwen needed him for something. So the check had been handed off to him and he'd get to bring it to Laura.

Other than a brief glimpse of her sitting on the front porch, drinking her coffee, before they left for the job, he hadn't seen her since the taproom on Sunday. He'd been with his friends and she'd been with hers, but all he'd wanted to do was sit with her at a quiet table for two and get to know her better.

He wanted to take Laura out on a real date. That wouldn't be an easy thing to pull off in Stonefield, where a date night seemed to be supper at the diner and then… He didn't even know what. A walk through the town square, maybe.

He knew that wasn't entirely accurate, though. Since its opening, Sutton's Place Brewery & Tavern had become the date night hot spot in Stonefield, according to all the guys he'd worked with. And that was a problem for obvious reasons.

Then there was the fact asking Laura to go out with him could blow up his life. D&T had a huge area around Stonefield pretty much locked down, except for a few one-man operations. If Lane got pissed enough to fire him, he was going to be unemployed in an apartment he'd just moved into—which was owned by people who were practically family to both the Thompsons and the Suttons. Hell, even the only good place to get a beer was owned by people who might be pissed off if he made a move on Laura.

By the time he parked his truck in front of the

garage, his gut was in knots. He sent her a text message telling her he'd be up in a few minutes with a check, and then he went into the garage to clean himself up as much as he could in the shop sink. Another hot and sweaty day. While the frigid days of winter weren't much more fun, there was a sweet spot where he really loved working outside, and that was October.

A reply message told him Laura was in the office and he could come in whenever he was ready.

He didn't feel ready, but he did want to see her, so he headed toward the house. He rapped twice on the doorjamb because it still didn't feel right not to, and then he walked in and made his way to the office. The house was quiet, and he realized he hadn't seen Evie's Jeep in the driveway. If Laura was babysitting Becca, she might be napping, so he made sure to walk softly to her office.

When he peeked in, he could see the playpen and swing were empty. Laura was sitting at her desk with her bare feet resting on the crossbar. She had her chin propped on her left hand, and with her right, she was clicking her mouse through a game of solitaire on the computer screen.

"Working hard?" he teased, and she spun the chair to face him.

Seeing Laura made the frustrations of the day fall away, and he just savored looking at her for a moment. Her hair was in that messy bun on top of her head that he always wanted to pull free so it could tumble over his hands. Her cheeks were pink from being startled, and they matched the long T-shirt she wore over leggings. And the way her eyes softened and her mouth curved when she saw him shot pleasure through his body.

"Believe it or not, my role in this company is a lot easier than yours," she said, laughing as she turned to close out the game.

"Yours has a lot more math. I'll stick to running the chain saw." He walked over and reached past her to set the check on her desk.

While he was leaned over, she turned slightly and looked up at him. They froze there—not touching, but *so* close—without moving, and in her eyes, he could see a mirror of everything he was feeling. Their breathing seemed to sync, and he watched her lips part as she stared at his mouth.

He forced himself to back up so he wasn't hovering over her, but, as though they were connected by an invisible string, she rose to her feet and took a step away from her chair. Before he could reach for her, she pressed her fingers to her mouth and slowly shook her head.

"What are we doing, Riley McLaughlin?"

"I'm doing everything in my power *not* to do anything, but being around you seems to make me pretty powerless."

"You are too young for me."

It was his turn to shake his head. "Nope. The flip

side of that coin would be that you're too old for me, and I can tell you that is absolutely not true."

She laughed softly, her cheeks pink. "You know, people around here think you're younger than you actually are. They've decided you're the same age as Lane and Case."

He quirked an eyebrow at her. "Actually, Case is close to my age, I guess, since he's between Lane and me. And I also think it doesn't matter."

She barked out a laugh. "Easy for the younger man to say."

"I've spent the whole day trying to figure out a way to ask you out on a date without blowing up my life."

Her eyes widened. "A date? Flirting is one thing, but—"

"Flirting?" He moved a little closer to her, unable to help himself. "You think I'm just flirting with you?"

"You have *definitely* been flirting with me."

"Let me kiss you and I'll prove that, one, I'm not playing, and two, the dates on our birth certificates have absolutely no bearing on how much I want you."

"I don't want to blow up your life," she whispered.

"If I don't kiss you, *I* might literally blow up."

"There are *so* many reasons why you shouldn't kiss me."

He closed the distance between them, but he wouldn't kiss her until she wanted it, so he trailed his fingertips from the back of her hand up her arm. "But there's one very good reason I *should* kiss you."

She tilted her head back so she could see his face. "And what's that?"

"I think I'll die if I don't." He'd never put everything—like his dignity—on the line trying to kiss a woman before, but, then again, he couldn't remember ever wanting to this badly in his adult life.

"How can I say no to that?"

He sucked in a breath when she placed her hand on his waist and then slid it to his back to pull him closer.

Riley cupped the back of her neck and slowly lowered his mouth to hers. He wanted to pounce—to devour her until he forgot his own name—but he wanted this kiss too much to rush through it.

Her lips were soft, and he wanted to moan with pleasure, but held it back, not wanting to push too hard, too soon. When her tongue brushed over his bottom lip, though, he couldn't hold back the sound.

He deepened the kiss, still cupping her neck with one hand. The other, he ran over her hip. The flimsy fabric of the T-shirt and leggings tempted him to feel the curve of her ass in his hands, but he behaved himself for now and caressed her back instead.

Laura leaned into him, stretching up onto her toes and matching his hunger. Her fingertips bit into the muscles of his lower back. When she nipped at his lip, he groaned and crumpled the back of her shirt in his fist.

He kissed her until he couldn't take it anymore—until he had to stop or he was going to go too far. He'd asked for one kiss and that was all he'd take. But what a kiss it was.

When he broke it off, Laura made a quiet sound of protest that almost made him change his mind. But he stepped back and looked into eyes as dazed as he felt.

"You're definitely not playing," she whispered.

"And there's no doubt I want you," he said after clearing his throat. The way her body had pressed against his, there was no way she could have missed the hardening evidence of it.

"No doubt at all." Her mouth curved into a smile that did nothing to cool him off.

"So can I take you out on a date? Go see a movie with me this weekend."

"Evie's going to be at the taproom Saturday night, so I have Becca."

"What about Friday night? I can run home and clean up, and then we can drive to the city. We can grab something quick to eat on the way."

She wanted to. He could see it, and he hoped she could see how much he wanted her to say yes. "There's a romantic comedy playing I've wanted to see."

He got the impression she was testing him somehow, but this was an easy one. "Laughing and falling in love? That sounds perfect."

She laughed and pushed at his shoulder. "Said no guy ever."

"I happen to like laughing and I like love. And I don't care what we watch. I just want to watch it with you."

"How are we going to...?" She stopped. Sighed. Gave him a sheepish smile. "I don't think you picking me up at my door is a great idea."

This was the part he didn't like, but she was worth it. "If you don't mind driving, I'll walk to the town square and you can pick me up."

The relief in her eyes didn't hide how much she also hated the sneaking-around part. "I don't mind driving."

"Then it's a date," he said, and then left before she could talk herself out of it.

"That was an utter waste of time," Ellen muttered as they left the library.

Laura agreed. "Meetings like that usually are."

"The agenda was very clear. We need to paint the gazebo in the town square, so tell us why that isn't covered by the town's maintenance budget. Ninety minutes later and we still don't know."

"I think budget meetings—any town meetings, really—should have moderators with water guns. If you go off topic and use the time to rant about a streetlight out, you get squirted."

"And we got a bonus lecture from the fire chief about shoveling out hydrants. It's July. I feel like that lecture could wait until Chelsea breaks out the pumpkin spice at the coffee shop, at least."

They walked from the library to the thrift shop, occasionally stopping to say hi to others out and about. When they reached Sutton's Seconds, Laura was going to say goodbye and keep walking, but Ellen waved her in.

"We just got some cute winter clothes dropped off that should fit Becca. I put them aside, if you want to grab them."

Having a best friend who owned a really great thrift store wasn't a hardship at all, Laura thought as she followed her in. Mallory was sitting behind the counter, with Leeza in the sling. Technically, she was on maternity leave, but that wasn't really a thing when everybody in the family was self-employed. She hadn't been working in the thrift store, and Irish certainly wasn't letting her work in the taproom, but she was getting antsy in the house and had offered to watch the store so Ellen could attend the gazebo meeting. Usually she straightened shelves and re-arranged items so older things could get more visibility. There were always small repairs or minor mending to do on donations in the back room. But today she was just sitting behind the counter, scrolling on her phone.

"Perfect timing," Mallory said when they walked in. "She just decided to add some fragrance to the store."

Ellen wrinkled her nose. "You might be right. I think she *is* more disgusting than her brothers were."

"I'd suggest lighting a candle, but the store might

explode." Mallory slung the diaper bag over her shoulder. "I'm going to change her out back before we leave. I don't want her sitting in that in the car."

"And you don't want your car to stink," Ellen said, making them all laugh.

Once Mallory had taken her adorable stink bomb into the back room to deal with her diaper, Ellen pulled out the bag of winter clothes. They went through it together, making sure they both thought Becca would be able to wear them. Ellen had a good eye, so everything worked.

"It's too bad Becca and Leeza will be off seasons," Laura said. With a half a year between the cousins, they'd hit age milestones on opposite seasons. "Although Leeza's a lot longer than Becca was."

"We'll save everything. When the time comes, if Leeza can't use it, it'll hit the shelves at just the right time."

With the business of choosing clothes for their granddaughter concluded, Ellen put the bag on the end of the counter. Laura didn't bother offering to pay for half of the value, since they'd already gone several rounds about that one and Laura had lost every one of them. She had her ways of getting around Ellen, though, and she'd do another declutter run through her home and find some things to donate to the shop. She always managed to offset half the cost of anything they claimed for Becca, and she was pretty sure Ellen hadn't figured it out yet.

"Do you know if Riley needs anything for his

apartment?" Ellen asked, jerking Laura out of her thoughts. Hearing his name threw her off, and she hoped Ellen couldn't tell.

"I...don't know. I haven't seen it." Was there some reason Ellen thought she might have been in Riley's apartment? Maybe the looks they'd exchanged across the taproom hadn't gone as unnoticed as she'd hoped.

"I didn't know if he'd said anything while he was in the office."

"Not that I know of. And he had an apartment before, and Molly's is on the small side, so if anything, he might have stuff he needs to get rid of."

Ellen chuckled. "Good point. While I'm thinking of it, Lane's working the bar tomorrow night so Irish can take Mallory to the diner for supper. Not really a date night, but more of a give-her-a-break night. I'll be watching the boys and Leeza, if you want to come over and start watching that new series on Netflix everybody's talking about."

"I'm going out tomorrow night, so I won't be around." As soon as the words left her mouth, Laura wanted desperately to take them back. She should have said something else—anything else. Cleaning her oven. A meeting. Anything but *going out*.

"Oh, where are you going?"

"I'm...I'm going to see a movie."

Ellen's brow wrinkled. "Who are you going with?"

"I..." Laura had no idea what to say. For the last few years, the only answer to that question was Ellen herself. She couldn't·say she was going alone, because that would be weird, and also because she'd have no way out if her friend invited herself along, and she might. Gwen would watch Leeza and the boys if she asked. Laura could make up a fake man, but she didn't want to lie to her best friend.

"Oh...*oh*!" Ellen's eyes widened and she took a step back. "Evie was talking about a movie she wants to see, and Lane said Riley mentioned he was going to see it tomorrow night. What are the chances the two of you just decided to make the half-hour drive to the movie theater on the same night?"

Laura wanted to say something quippy and then change the subject, but words had abandoned her. This was happening and she couldn't see a way out.

"Laura Thompson, are you dating Riley McLaughlin?"

"No, I am not," she said quickly. "We're friends."

"Friends going on a date."

"You and I go to the movies together. Are *we* dating?"

"You tell Lane when you're going to the movies with me." Ellen put her hands on her hips and tilted her head. "Did you tell him you're going to the movies with Riley?"

"I don't have to tell Lane where I'm going or who I'm going with. I don't always tell him when you and I go see a movie or go thrifting or whatever we're doing."

"So, *no*. Lane doesn't know the new guy and his mother are going on a date."

To her horror, tears sprang to Laura's eyes, and she tried to blink them away. She almost never cried.

"Honey." The annoyance and sarcasm were dropped as Ellen peered into her face. "What's going on?"

What was going on? She'd thought maybe she could go on one date with Riley without anybody knowing, and she should have known better. Now it was all going to blow up, just as he'd feared, and it was her fault for not being able to resist him.

"Please don't tell anybody," she whispered.

"I won't tell a soul." Ellen hooked her pinkie around Laura's. "Lucy and Lucy forever, remember? But tell me, because, yes, I was shocked, but I love you, and if this is upsetting you, I want to know."

"It's not. I just… It's complicated. He works for my son, Ellen. And my nephew. It's a little weird, and he just moved here away from his family to start this job."

"And he's young."

"He's not *that* young." The tears glimmered again. "But see? Everybody will call me a cougar. People will *talk*."

"I don't think he's young enough for you to be called a cougar. And nobody's going to talk, because I'm the only one who knows. Go to the movies and get that itch scratched."

Laura groaned, shaking her head.

"I'm serious," Ellen said. "If you're going to have a fling, it might as well be with a younger guy. We're old enough now so having a fling with an older guy could still be fun, but the fun wouldn't go on and on, if you know what I mean."

"Ellen Sutton." But Laura laughed and was able to wipe the moisture from her eyes, as Leeza's squawking told them Mallory was on her way back to the front of the store.

"I hope you didn't leave that diaper in the trash can back there," Ellen told her daughter.

"Of course not." She held up a bundle that looked like it had four or five plastic bags wrapped around it. "I was going to put it in the diaper bag, but I have snacks in there. For me, not for Leeza, obviously. And I don't want to put it in the car, because you know I'll forget it, and then I'll have to set the car on fire in the driveway. I'm going to toss it in the can out front."

"Not the can right out front," Ellen said. "At least two down the sidewalk, please."

Laura would have liked to leave before Mallory, ensuring there would be no more conversation about her and Riley, but Mallory was already halfway through the door.

"'Bye, Laura. I'll see you at home, Mom."

"Okay, back to the Riley situation," Ellen said as soon as the door closed behind her daughter.

"We're just going to a movie, and I have to get home. I'm expecting a call from the power company."

Ellen rolled her eyes. "You always use them as an excuse when you want to go home. But listen—

I want to hear all about how the movie goes…and I don't mean I want a review of the movie."

"I know what you mean, and it won't be an exciting story."

"I'll be disappointed if it's not," Ellen said as Laura picked up the bag of clothes for Becca and headed for the door. "If I'm going to keep secrets for you, Laura Thompson, at least make them good ones."

Chapter Six

There's a debate raging in Stonefield, though we're not sure which residents kicked it off: Is a pizza without sauce still a pizza? Or is it a round cheesy bread? We asked Stonefield House of Pizza to weigh in and here's their response: "We'll tell you the same thing we've told the many people who've called—we don't judge pizzas (except that one time we got a request for a tuna-fish-and-pineapple pizza) and we don't define them. Order your pizza the way you want it, and we'll make it for you. (Unless it involves tuna. We'll do anything for pizza, but we won't do that.)" If you want to weigh in, here's a poll! We'll report back in a few days.
                    —Stonefield Gazette *Facebook Page*

Riley felt so conspicuous walking around the town square, he wondered why they hadn't just told Lane they were going to see a movie. That seemed like less of a big deal than Lane getting a phone call telling him his mother was spotted picking up a guy on the side of Main Street.

Then her red Subaru crossover pulled up next to him, and he slid into the passenger seat as quickly as he could. She was laughing and that made it worth the risk.

"This is so ridiculous," she said as she sped away from the curb.

"Can't argue with that." He found the seat adjuster to give himself a little more leg room and then buckled his seat belt. "Kind of fun, though."

It wasn't until he was settled and turned to face her that it hit him. Her hair was down. It fell in a dark, thick mass of waves just past her shoulders, and he ached to feel it slide between his fingers.

"I knew you'd have gorgeous hair," he told her, his hands clenched so he wouldn't give in to the temptation to touch it. "It's always out of your way when you're working, and I've been dying to see it down."

"It's so much easier just to pile it up all messy on my head with a scrunchie, especially now that we have Becca. As you learned, she has quite a grip."

"The messy pile is cute," he said sincerely.

They made small talk while she drove. They talked about movies and books. Music. They had pretty different taste in music, though they both had a love of classic country music.

He wisely didn't tell Laura his liking for old country songs came from his mother. He'd noticed the one thing they weren't talking about was her family, except for the occasional mention of Becca. There was no talk of Lane or Case or the tree service, and he was perfectly okay with that.

They didn't want to miss getting good seats at the theater, so they hit a drive-through and ate fast food in the car.

"Am I impressing you with this date yet?" he asked, nudging her elbow with his.

She held up a fry. "This is a perfect first date, actually. Do you know how often I wish we could get a fast-food place in Stonefield? All the time. At least once a week, mostly for the fries."

"Good to know."

"I got the diner to serve shoestring fries for a while, but other customers complained." She shrugged. "And they weren't as good as these."

"Nothing worse than being disappointed by French fries."

She laughed and popped the fry into her mouth. He took a bite of his burger and leaned back in the seat, happier than he'd been in a long time. He was with a beautiful woman. She was laughing. And they'd really come through with the extra pickles on his burger. Life didn't get much better.

They were sitting in the dimly-lit theater, wait-

ing for the previews to start, when she leaned close
to him. "I should probably tell you that Ellen knows
I'm here with you."

He almost dropped the bucket of popcorn. "By
Ellen, you mean the mother-in-law of *both* of my
bosses?"

"She figured it out." She took a small handful of
the popcorn. "And it's partly your fault, because you
told Lane and Evie you were going to the movies. So
when I told Ellen I was going to the movies, which
I'm not sure I've done without her since I was about
twenty years old, she knew something was up."

"Okay." He munched popcorn and stared at the
really obnoxious cartoon on the screen urging them
to silence their cell phones while he tried to mentally draw lines from Ellen directly to all the people who could be upset with him for taking Laura
to the movies. He was going to need a bigger mental whiteboard.

"She won't tell anybody."

He chuckled. "I haven't gotten the impression
that's how the Sutton-Thompson-etcetera greater
family tree works."

"Usually everybody would know by now, but she's
my ride or die. She won't tell anybody, though she's
not happy about it."

"Not happy that she can't tell anybody or not
happy that you're here with me?"

The music swelled as the previews started, and
Laura smiled and waved a hand at him as if to tell

him not to worry about it. If she wasn't concerned, he probably didn't need to be, so he put Ellen and the rest of them out of his mind and concentrated on just being present in this moment.

The movie was engaging and fun, and Laura laughed a lot. Even though he didn't love the movie, he did love watching her enjoy it, and when the lights came up in the theater, her eyes were sparkling.

"That was a fun movie, don't you think?" she asked after they'd discarded the empty popcorn bucket and soda cups and were making their way outside.

"I enjoyed it. It was funnier than I expected."

"The first time I saw the trailer, I knew I wanted to see it, but I figured I'd forget about it. Usually it's in the theaters for a while, but it's a long drive, so Ellen and I only go maybe once a year, if that. By the time they hit the streaming services, I've forgotten about them."

"I love watching movies on the big screen, so you let me know when you see a trailer."

"Even if it's another romantic comedy?" she teased.

Her hand brushed his and he caught it, threading his fingers through hers as they walked. "Sure. I'm not picky."

"You said you like horror movies, but I'll be honest. I don't know if I could watch a horror movie with you."

"Even if we watched it on television, so you can hide under the blanket when you get scared?"

She laughed and tugged at his hand so he looked at her. "I'm old enough to know why boys watch horror movies with girls and get them to hide under the blanket. I know what's under there."

Riley hadn't been thinking that, but now he was going to have a hard time thinking about anything else. "Damn. It's tough when you've figured out all of our tricks."

Once they were out of the city, Laura drove easily with her left hand, and her right was clasped in his and rested on the center console. She talked about her favorite parts of the movie and he was happy to listen. He was glad she'd genuinely had a good time, because that meant she might do it again. Maybe a picnic, he thought. Something private, but not requiring so much driving time.

When they got back to Stonefield, he expected her to drop him near the square, but she didn't stop.

"I can drop you off. It's dark and the streetlight's out on the corner."

"Are you going to come to a complete stop, or should I be prepared to tuck and roll?"

"I'll stop. And it would be strange—and therefore notable—if I picked you up to take you somewhere, but it's not all that strange for me to have run into you and given you a ride home. So not only do you not have to tuck and roll, but you don't need to put a blanket over your head."

"I guess it would be strange—and therefore notable—if I kissed you thoroughly to thank you for the ride?"

"I'd hate for you to set a precedent like that. We like to be neighborly here, and I give people rides fairly often."

He laughed. "Guys will be stealing their own plug wires all over this town, trying to come up with an excuse to need a ride."

"That's all I need." She stopped the car near the corner, though she didn't put it in Park. "Just so you know, I would have let you kiss me good-night."

"I'll owe it to you." He opened the door. "Stop by tomorrow and you can collect on it."

She laughed. "Maybe. Good night, Riley."

"Thanks for tonight. Good night, Laura." He closed the door quietly, pushing in on it to make sure it was latched, and the car was rolling before he'd stood up straight.

He hurried into the shadows of the garage, hoping nobody was paying attention, which didn't seem likely. But right now, he didn't even care. If going out with Laura cost him his new job and his new apartment, he'd roll with that.

She was definitely worth it.

"Hiring Riley McLaughlin was the smartest move Case and I have made in years."

Her son's voice carried through the downstairs, and Laura turned to the stove to hide the guilty flush she was afraid was visible. Also so the bacon wouldn't burn, but mostly so the heat from the hot grease would offer an excuse for her pink cheeks when Lane walked into the kitchen carrying Becca. Evie was right behind him.

"I'm glad he's working out," her daughter-in-law said. "I've heard the guys all like him, too."

"They do. Good morning, Mom."

She heard the familiar sounds of the high chair as he fit Becca's legs into it and then buckled her in. "Good morning."

"I'm pretty sure it was my turn to cook breakfast," Evie said as she took the juice out of the fridge.

"I was up early and I don't mind."

Lane and Evie continued chatting about Riley while they set the table and prepared some rice cereal for Becca. Lane was telling his wife about the dynamic of him, Case and Riley, and how it felt almost as though the three of them had been running the company together for years.

And all Laura could think about, as she transferred the bacon to a paper-towel-lined plate and set the eggs to scrambling, was how devastating it would be for her son—and for the tree service—if she ruined it for everybody by getting into a potentially very messy situation with Riley.

"You're quiet today," Evie said when they were almost finished eating. "Everything okay?"

"Of course." She forced a brightness into her voice she didn't feel. "I have a lot of errands today, so I was just sorting them in my head."

"Oh, are you stopping by the thrift shop?" Evie asked. "I have some things Becca's outgrown that Mallory doesn't want for Leeza, and I keep forgetting to drop them off. Or even put them in my Jeep so I can leave them at the house."

Laura hadn't been planning to go to Sutton's Seconds, because she wasn't sure she wanted to visit Ellen while she was so tied up in knots over Riley, but it would look odd if she said no. "I can drop them off for you. Are you sure you don't want to hold on to them for a while, though?"

Lane chuckled when Evie shook her head with enthusiasm. "I'm not ready to think about another one yet, Laura. Maybe next year. *Maybe.* And there's no sense in it cluttering up the house when there are always baby clothes flowing through the thrift shop."

"You're right about that," she said, standing and carrying her dishes to the sink. "Better they go to somebody who can use them now instead of sitting in a box in your closet."

"We'll clean up, Mom." Lane sighed when Becca used her tongue to push out the spoonful of cereal he'd just fed her. "This girl is finicky, and that definitely doesn't come from my side of the family."

Evie laughed. "She's not finicky. She's just messy, and she *definitely* gets that from her daddy."

Laura kissed the top of Becca's head—practically the only spot free of cereal—and left them to their banter. She took her time doing her usual Saturday morning chores. She started a load of laundry and cleaned her bathroom. Then she added a few toiletries she was running low on to her shopping list.

It was all fairly routine, which left her mind free to consider the problem of Riley. She'd woken up thinking about going to his apartment and getting that good-night kiss she was owed.

But the conversation between Lane and Evie gave her pause. So far, she and Riley had only shared one kiss and a trip to the movie theater. Despite the attraction burning between them, they could walk it back and go back to a friendly, professional relationship. Maybe.

The truth was, though, that she didn't want to. If she took everybody else and the company out of the equation and only considered herself, she wanted this. She wanted *him*, and she was a little bit tired of only doing what was best for everybody else.

She let that defiance get her out the door—snagging the bag of clothes on her way—and into her car. And it carried her through town until she slowed at the corner where the funeral home sat.

There was no way to hide her car. If she parked, anybody who bothered to notice would assume she'd stopped by to visit Amanda, or maybe Molly on the other side of the fence. But the Cyrs women would know she hadn't knocked on their doors.

That defiant focus on herself was fading fast, so before she lost it totally, she parked behind Riley's truck and went up the stairs to his door. Her heart was hammering in her chest as she knocked, but as soon as he opened the door, the racing pulse became less about the other residents of Stonefield and a lot more about the sweet smile he greeted her with.

"I wasn't sure you'd come," he said, stepping back to let her in.

"I wasn't sure, either." There was a tremor in her voice, and she cleared her throat as she glanced around the small apartment. "You didn't paint it?"

He looked around the cheerful yellow walls, but apparently he didn't see anything wrong with them. "Why would I paint it?"

"I don't know. Molly's aesthetic can be…a lot."

"I like it. It's nice and bright. And it's hard to be grumpy when you're surrounded by sunshine."

She laughed, shaking her head. "I have a hard time picturing you being grumpy. You seem very… even-tempered and positive."

"That's usually me, but I have my moments."

"Everybody does." Now that she was here, alone with him in a place where she didn't have to worry about somebody walking in at any moment, she wasn't sure what to do with herself.

She was so out of practice at this dating thing. Or maybe it was deeper than that, because she hadn't felt these kinds of nerves the last few times she'd gone out with a man. There was a distinct possibility the fact she was trembling with anticipation and didn't know what to do with her hands was due to the specific man standing in front of her right now.

"I owe you a good-night kiss," he said, moving

closer. When she blushed, he chuckled. "Did you think I'd forget?"

"I wasn't sure," she admitted.

He hooked his arm around her waist and pulled her close. "There was no way I could forget, since I've done nothing but think about it since I got out of your car last night. I thought about kissing you for the rest of the night. I dreamed about it. And kissing you was the first thing I thought about when I opened my eyes this morning."

If she'd managed to scrape together even a smidgen of resolve to resist this man, it would have melted away under the heat in his gaze as he said all the right words in a low, husky voice.

"Me, too," she confessed in a whisper.

When his mouth claimed hers, Laura's hands suddenly knew what to do with themselves again. One slid up his back while the other went to his hair. She threaded her fingers through the soft strands, and they tightened there as his tongue danced over hers.

For a moment, she regretted coming here in the afternoon, because if she was going to end up naked in his bed, she would have preferred it not be in broad daylight. But he put a hand on her hip, hauling her up hard against his body, and she stopped caring.

His kiss was hard and demanding, and she moaned against his lips. His fingertips pressed harder into her hip for a few seconds before he lifted his hand to cup the back of her neck. She loved the way he did that—the heat and pressure of it—and her only reservation about getting naked at this point was that it meant taking his hand away.

A hard knock on the door ended the kiss abruptly, startling them away from each other, and Laura decided she really didn't like whoever was on the other side of that door. After giving her a look that mirrored her frustration at the interruption, Riley walked across the room and opened the door to reveal Amanda Cyrs on the other side.

"Hi," she said, her gaze bouncing between Riley and Laura as if she was watching a fast-paced Ping-Pong match. "I hope I'm not interrupting."

Laura didn't even know what to say. Her brain seemed to have frozen along with her body, and she couldn't come up with a lie to fill the silence. Maybe because she hated lying, and she and Amanda had been friends for a long time. But not pinkie-swear, take-it-to-the-grave friends like she and Ellen were.

"Of course not," Riley said smoothly, stepping back to invite Amanda in. "I forgot to turn in some paperwork yesterday and Laura had an errand in town, so she offered to pick it up."

"Oh, that's nice of you," she said to Laura, and then she looked around as if searching for the paperwork in question.

"What can I do for you?" Riley asked, with maybe a touch of an edge to his voice.

"I saw Laura's car and she wasn't at Molly's, and I need to find out if she'll head the new committee we're starting to get that gazebo painted."

Friend or not, Laura felt a flash of anger. That was a ridiculously flimsy excuse. Amanda had seen her car and wanted to know what she was doing up here with Riley, which was none of her damn business. "Between the tree service and Becca, I don't really have time to head any committees right now, but I appreciate you thinking of me."

Amanda's disappointment was obvious, and Laura wondered if it was because she hadn't managed to foist unpaid labor on her, or if she'd been hoping to find something far more scandalous going on when she knocked on the door. Another ten minutes or so and there might have been, but she'd definitely killed the mood.

"I guess I'll ask Ellen, then," Amanda said, and Laura barely managed to keep from snorting. "Sorry to have bothered you, and I'll let you get back to your…paperwork."

Once she was gone, Riley leaned against the closed door with a scowl. "I've never lived in a small town before. Is it always so…suffocating?"

"It can feel pretty claustrophobic at times, for sure. I'd say she means well, because she usually does, but today she's straight-up fishing for gossip."

"I kind of wish I'd held on to my old apartment for a little bit longer."

"I've thought that, too," she confessed, and he pushed away from the door with a growl.

"Now I guess she'll be spying from behind a curtain to see how long you stay."

Laura sighed. "Probably."

Running his hand through his hair, he looked at her with his mouth set in a grim line. "I'm almost forty years old, Laura. I'm not into games. And I'm certainly not into being somebody you're ashamed of dating publicly."

"No." She stepped closer to him. "I'm not ashamed, Riley, and you know it. Do I want people to call me a cougar? No. But that's not it. You're not the only one who's worried about how Lane will react. He was just talking over breakfast about how much they value you, so we both have reasons we don't want the entire town talking about us."

He took her hand, threading his fingers through hers. "I know. I'm sorry. I'm just really frustrated because I like you, Laura. I want to see you and go out to dinner with you. Take a walk in the town square. Have you over without my landlord peeking in the windows."

"I know. I'm frustrated, too." Amanda's visit had definitely put a damper on things, and knowing she was watching for Laura to leave was enough to keep the flame from rekindling. "I should go. But we'll... I should go."

She pulled her hand free just in case he was of a mind to pull her back in for a goodbye kiss. If his lips touched hers again, she'd be lost and Amanda would be on the phone with Ellen and who even knew who else before they stopped for a breath. It would go downhill from there.

"We can't will away whatever this is," Riley said as she headed for the door.

"I know." If it was possible, she would have managed it already.

"Here, take this," he said, and she turned back to see him holding out two pieces of paper. "I told Amanda you were picking up paperwork."

She took them and glanced down to see they were blank sheets of printer paper. She spotted a laptop on his coffee table as she looked around, but she didn't see a printer.

"Two of my nieces and one of my nephews love drawing, so I learned a long time ago having blank paper, crayons and *washable* markers on hand is a good idea," he explained.

She smiled because he was clearly a great uncle. But the next thought—he'd make a wonderful father—ruined her mood even more than Amanda had.

"Thanks for these," she said, heading for the door.

"Laura." She stopped, but didn't turn around. "I know I probably won't see you again until Monday, but I'll be thinking about you every minute between now and then."

Her breath caught, but she still didn't let herself turn back. Instead, she nodded. "Me, too."

And then she left before he could say anything else. It would be so easy for him to make her forget all the reasons she should stay out of his bed, but the papers in her hand kept her focused on what was probably the most important one—even more impor-

tant than the tree service. Riley was almost forty—
the age so many men realized it was time to settle
down with a wife and have some babies.

And Laura had been there, done that, and she
wasn't doing it again.

Chapter Seven

The Badges For Backpacks Drive officially kicks off tomorrow—Stonefield PD versus Stonefield FD! Drop your school supplies at the police or fire stations during regular business hours, or leave items at the library and town hall, where each has a PD blue box and an FD red box. We don't yet know what the prize will be for the department that collects the most school supplies, but we're looking forward to watching those donation boxes fill up!
—Stonefield Gazette *Facebook Page*

By Monday afternoon, barely forty-eight hours after leaving his apartment, Laura had almost talked herself back into sleeping with Riley.

Not that she should be making any decisions after two nights in a row of more tossing and turning than sleeping. She'd lain in bed with her eyes closed and her body aching for his touch, trying to force back the provocative images filling her mind with the list of reasons to resist him.

It was like a revolving door that never stopped spinning. Lane. The tree service. His age. Gossip. *Her* age. The fact he should be starting to think about settling down when she was already *very* settled. And back to Lane.

Then those images of Riley naked and kissing her body would sneak through, and she'd get frustrated all over again.

If he wanted a wife and kids, he should be out looking for a potential bride. If he preferred to spend his time kissing her, that was on him. She wasn't responsible for his life choices.

The question in her mind was how to give in to the passion simmering between her and Riley without causing drama with everybody else in her life.

She couldn't exactly ask him in to cuddle on the couch while they watched television—or pretended to. Yes, it was her home, but it was also Lane's home. If he came home and found his mother making out with a guy on the couch, he'd be shocked. And it would definitely be awkward for everybody. Men had been in the house a few times over the years, for dinner, but she'd saved intimacy for behind closed doors—the *guy's* door.

But if Lane walked in and found her making out with Riley? There was a good chance that shock and awkwardness would give way to anger. She definitely didn't want to get caught making out with Riley on the couch, but she couldn't invite him in and hustle him straight to her bedroom.

Okay, so she could—and she was pretty sure he wouldn't mind—but she wasn't sure she'd have the nerve.

And she would have driven the forty minutes to his place, but now he lived in Molly's old apartment and, as they'd learned on Saturday, Amanda was watching. Laura was starting to feel like a teenager again, sneaking around and trying to find a way to be alone with her boyfriend.

Of course, doing that had gotten her a husband, a baby and a life that wasn't as fun and romantic as Joe had led her to believe it would be. She had no regrets because she'd gotten Lane out of it—and now Becca—but she'd learned a lot over the course of her marriage.

She'd learned she liked being free to do as she pleased. After growing up with an extremely strict father, she went straight to a husband who'd seemingly learned about gender roles in a previous century.

Of course she'd mourned Joe. She *had* loved him, and he'd been a good father to Lane. But once she'd gotten her feet under herself, emotionally, she'd started feeling…free. Free to watch all the shows her friends talked about, but that Joe hadn't liked. Free to eat leftover pizza cold from the fridge for Sunday breakfast.

Lane and Evie had moved in with her for the first time shortly after the funeral, and between his grief and the crumbling of his marriage, Laura had done her best to make the house feel like the home he'd grown up in. But she hadn't let herself go from taking care of her father to taking care of her husband to taking care of her son. Lane did his share of the housekeeping, including half the cooking, and if he didn't like what she made when it was her turn, he could drive himself over to the diner and have whatever they were serving.

The front door closing jerked her attention away from the spreadsheet she'd been ignoring while thinking about Riley.

It was a little early to be him coming inside—plus, he hadn't sent a text—but it could be. Or it could be any of the others, but even the possibility it could be Riley was enough to quicken her pulse.

When Ellen poked her head in, Laura had to fight to not look disappointed. Instead, she smiled brightly and waved for her friend to enter the office. "I didn't know you were stopping by."

Ellen shrugged and sat in the armchair. "Callan's trying to get a chess club going at the library because— according to him—not enough young people know how to play. I told him I'd come, so I came to drag you with me."

"Is he ever *not* at the library? What does Molly think of another club?"

"She's helping him with it. You know she loves mixing things up."

Laura laughed. "Molly is terrible at chess."

"Callan said she's a great cheerleader, though." Ellen shrugged. "I didn't ask."

"I'm not a huge fan of chess. I don't know."

"It'll be fun, unless you have plans with your young man."

She rolled her eyes. "One, he's not mine. Two, I don't have plans with anybody tonight. And three—with a star and in bold print—he's not *that* young."

"Laura, I ran into him at the taproom last night, and you're dating somebody so young he called me *ma'am*."

"Again, we're not dating—exactly. And he's polite. He was raised to call women 'ma'am.'"

"Oh, really? Does he call *you* 'ma'am'?"

Heat colored Laura's cheeks. "No, he doesn't."

"So, do you call him *sir*?" Evie asked from the doorway, and Laura and Ellen both jumped.

Laura could tell by her daughter-in-law's grin and her tone that the innuendo had been deliberate, and she blushed harder.

"Evie!" Ellen exclaimed, so she knew her friend hadn't missed it, either.

"Obviously we didn't hear you come in," Laura said, trying to sound calm. "Is Lane with you?"

Please say no, she thought, hoping the desperate thought didn't show on her face.

"No, it's just me and Becca," Evie said, and then she laughed at Laura's sigh of relief. "It's not a big deal."

"It's a very big deal. He doesn't want things to be weird with Lane. And I don't want people to think I'm... He's younger than me."

She snorted. "Not that much. But I have a question. Where are you hanging out? I haven't seen him doing a walk of shame through our kitchen, and I'm pretty sure Molly would have said something if you were hanging out at his place, because it's Molly. She can't *not* say something."

"We're not hanging out. We went to the movie theater because it's far enough away, so we wouldn't be tripping over people Lane knows." Laura shook her head. "I did stop by his apartment on Saturday, and within a few minutes Amanda knocked on the door. She wanted to ask me about heading the gazebo committee."

"Oh, that's subtle," Ellen said, taking the baby from Evie. "That committee hasn't even been approved yet. We've been friends a long time, but sometimes she gets on my last nerve."

"Riley told her I'd dropped off some paperwork, so I had to leave right after she did, because you know she was going to watch and see when I left."

"You know, when Lane and I go camping, you're

going to have the entire house to yourself for a long weekend," Evie said.

Heat flooded Laura's face, and she wished Evie had handed Becca to her instead of Ellen because she'd have a reason not to look at either of the women. "And what am I supposed to do? Tell him he can sneak into my bedroom after the other guys leave every day, and then when you come home, we go back to…driving an hour to be alone?"

"Or," Evie said, drawing the word out, "you could tell Lane you're dating Riley. Just a thought."

"And you think he's just going to be okay with it?" Laura scoffed.

"No," Evie responded. "Not at first. But he loves you, and he not only likes Riley, but he needs him. So once he's had a day or two to wrap his head around it, he'll be fine."

"I'm not willing to put Riley in that position."

"You could go on strike," Ellen said. "Case and Lane could handle things without you if they absolutely had to, but it would be a hot mess and they'd hate it. Case would make Lane come around."

"I don't want the conflict." Laura sighed. "I was so content with my life, too."

"Were you content or were you in a rut so deep, you convinced yourself you were content so you didn't have to get yourself out of it?" Evie asked.

"I'm *content*," she snapped, offended by the suggestion she was stuck in a rut—especially from her daughter-in-law. "I have an amazing, full life. I have a lovely home. I'm surrounded by family and friends, and I've been blessed with a beautiful granddaughter. What is it you think I should change?"

"Change? Nothing. But you could have all that and *also* have a smokin' hot younger guy taking care of you."

Everything in Laura recoiled at the words *taking care of you*.

She knew what that meant. Joe had taken care of her—he'd paid the bills with his job, so everything else was her job. He had to work all day, so she changed every one of Lane's diapers, day and night. He had to work all day, so she did all the housekeeping *and* the bookkeeping. She answered the phones. They ate what he wanted, when he wanted. They only watched shows he liked. He'd never demanded it. She was just thankful she had him to take care of her and arranged their lives to suit him.

In Laura's experience, having a man to take care of her meant her taking care of literally everything else. She preferred to take care of herself, thank you very much. She ate what she wanted, when she wanted. She only watched shows she liked, and if she wanted to stay up half the night watching one, it was nobody's business but hers.

She didn't want to be taken care of.

"I still think you should tell Lane," Evie said. "I won't. I promise. But you should because you deserve to have some fun in your life."

She did deserve to have fun. And now that Evie

had reminded her they were going camping, it was all she could think about. She was going to be alone in the house for four nights.

Maybe she didn't have to be alone, after all. But having a man in her space was a big thing. She hadn't had a man in her bedroom since Joe died, and she didn't mind that. It was *hers*, and she liked the ceiling fan on, hot or cold. She had her phone charger and a box of tissues and her hand cream on one nightstand and books on the other. They were both hers and she didn't want to share. She was never going to give up a part of herself for a man again.

But maybe one visiting temporarily wouldn't be a bad thing. Something to think about.

By late morning on Friday, Riley was exhausted from beating himself up for not being able to forget about Laura. It had been a week since they went to the movies, and that disastrous visit she'd made to his apartment the next day had been the last time he'd been alone with her.

It was too hard and he didn't know the right answer. It was easy to think they were adults and it didn't matter what anybody else thought. They shouldn't have to hide their attraction to each other. But since the idea of telling Lane made his stomach burn with anxiety, he knew it wasn't that easy.

Especially for her. He was frustrated, sure, and there was a possibility his job would suffer if he crossed the line with her. That would suck. But this was her *life*. It was easy for him to say he didn't care about the gossip because they weren't his friends and family. While he hoped it wouldn't always be the case, he wasn't a part of this community.

And Lane was his boss, but he was Laura's *son*. Case was her nephew. The stakes were so much higher for her if they got into a relationship and it didn't go over well.

But still, he couldn't stop thinking about her. He hadn't been wrong when he told her he would. And he'd thought he would get a few minutes with her yesterday when a customer had handed over a paper lunch bag of cash—along with a lecture on the evils of banks—but when he'd walked into the office, he found her with Bruce, going over some bids.

He'd had to stand there and make small talk with Bruce while Laura counted out the cash. Then she'd smiled and thanked him, and that was it. There was nothing he could do but tell her to have a good evening and walk out.

"Not like you to get lost in thought on the job," Lane said, startling him.

And there was the anxiety and guilt churning his gut again. "Sorry. You ready to cut?"

"Yeah. Neil and Shane just have to move the chipper out of the way and we'll be ready."

There weren't many jobs that required five of them, but it was the kind of job with multiple trees and a few challenges, so it was more men and one day, or fewer men and more days. They had a tight schedule in the summer, so Lane had trusted Irish to handle the brewery and had come in on a Friday.

"I haven't heard from Mom yet," Lane said, pulling out his phone and frowning at it—presumably at the lack of notifications. "I expected her to be back by now."

Riley had seen her back out of the driveway that morning and it had seemed odd. He'd never seen her leave the house before the crews left. "Where did she go?"

"Almost to the Maine border to get a part for the other chipper. She's gone there a few times before, so I know she didn't get lost."

"But she should be back by now?" The anxiety came from a new place now, and it was even more potent. If Lane was worrying, there was something to worry about.

"Maybe she's been back for an hour and didn't text me. That happens." Lane shrugged, sliding the phone back into his pocket. "Or there was a new thrift store on the way, or yard sales. Or a yarn store. Looks like the guys are ready, so we're up."

Riley had to put Laura out of his mind while he was up in the bucket, running the chain saw. It was one thing to risk himself, but it was a complicated drop, and he didn't want to screw up and get one of the other guys hurt.

With the hardest of the trees taken care of, they took a lunch break. There was a lot of small talk about trucks and fishing, and sneaking bits of sandwiches to Boomer. Then they cleaned up and prepared to go back to work.

He was laughing at one of Shane's *very* tall tales when Lane's phone rang. He looked at the screen, smiled, and then took a few steps away to answer it.

"Hey, Evie. What's up?"

After a few seconds of listening, the color drained from Lane's face. Riley stepped forward, ready to catch him if he fell—or at least make sure he didn't hit his head—but Case was already there.

Please, not the baby, Riley thought.

"Where are they taking her?" Lane asked, and Riley tensed. Since it was very unlikely any of the women in Lane's life were being arrested, somebody was in an ambulance. Becca's adorable face flashed in his mind again. "I'm leaving now. I'll be there as soon as I can."

Case had started moving as soon as Lane asked where they were going, and Riley helped him out. Case's stuff was transferred to Lane's truck, and after a hand gesture from his human, Boomer jumped up into the back seat.

Then Case tossed Riley his keys. "You're in charge. Get the job done and then take my truck back to the shop. If we're not back, just leave the keys in it."

When Lane lowered his phone, they both stopped to look at him. He blinked a couple of times, then shook his head. "Mom was in an accident."

Laura.

A swift, sharp sense of relief it wasn't Becca

washed over him before dread settled like a rock in his stomach. That was why Laura was late. She was hurt. The other two men were already in motion, heading toward Lane's truck, and he wanted to call after them—to ask Lane how bad it was—but it wasn't his place. His place was to keep the guys working and drive Case's truck back to the shop when the workday was over.

His place sucked.

Chapter Eight

We're passing along a statement from Chief Nelson on behalf of the Stonefield Fire Department: "We've seen an increase in calls about chipmunks in the walls of several houses on Poplar Road and, unless the chipmunks are running around with lit matches, that's not our job. Also, we've seen the sunflowers residents have planted to cheer up the neighborhood. They're pretty, but if you have sunflowers you have chipmunks."

—Stonefield Gazette *Facebook Page*

"This is ridiculous. I just want to go home."

"Mom." Lane blew out a breath and shook his head, which, as far as Laura was concerned, was the grown man version of a teen girl rolling her eyes. "They're working on your discharge papers and then you'll be able to go."

Laura wanted her chair, her book and a whole lot of quiet time. If she could lose herself in reading, maybe the split second she'd realized the dump truck wasn't going to stop at the stop sign would stop replaying in her mind like the worst GIF ever. It would be a long time before she forgot the sound of crunching metal and shattering glass, though.

She didn't need anybody to tell her how extraordinarily lucky she'd been. Her only injuries were a very mild concussion, soreness from her seat belt locking her against the seat, some light burning on her arms from the airbag deployment and a variety of aches and pains.

"You're really going to feel those tomorrow," her notably young doctor had told her of those aches and pains. "Especially at your age."

At her age? She was only forty-eight, thank you very much.

The ambulance had been overkill, too, but she'd been so shaken up after the impact, she'd gone along with whatever the EMTs told her. If it had taken them longer to arrive on the scene and she'd had time to get her wits about her, she would have called Ellen or Evie to come and drive her in to get checked out. Or she could have ridden in the police car with the other driver since he wasn't hurt, but, as the driver of a commercial dump truck, he had to go to the hospital and have a blood test to rule out driving under the influence.

"How is my car?" she asked, hoping to distract herself from how long it was taking for them to discharge her.

Lane snorted. "Pretty good except for the side that got hit by a dump truck."

Tears shimmered in her eyes, and she turned away so he wouldn't see them. Maybe it was just a ten-year-old Subaru, but it was *her* Subaru. It was paid off. She'd just put new tires on it last fall. The cup holder was just the right size for her favorite tumbler, and she had the console storage set up just the way she liked it.

"Mom, I'm sorry." Lane's arms wrapped around her shoulders and he rested his chin on her shoulder, so she must not have turned around fast enough. "I know you loved that car. If it could be fixed, you know I would get it done for you, but the insurance company is going to total it. There's no way the frame's not wrecked."

"I had my library tote in the back seat."

"Gwen picked up Case here and they went to get everything for you. And Vinnie put anything that might blow out in the cab of his truck before he hauled it onto the ramp, and he towed it back to his place. Your library books will be waiting for you at home."

"Did he get the part for the chipper?"

"Yes. Everything's taken care of, Mom. The only

thing you need to worry about is you." He started pacing again, tiny circles in the limited space he had. "I should text Evie and have her call the campground. Maybe they'll have an open spot later in the month."

She'd forgotten about their vacation. "You're not canceling your trip. You've been looking forward to it, and it was a miracle the campground had an opening. You've got Riley to handle things with Case, and the taproom's schedule is all figured out. That wasn't easy and we don't want to do it all over again, so just go."

They were borrowing Irish and Mallory's camper and spending a few days at a fun family campground. It had a ton of amenities, including a little splashing pool for babies that Becca would love. Laura *definitely* didn't want to be the reason they didn't go.

It had been fairly spur-of-the-moment, and Laura hadn't made up her mind yet what she was going to do about the fact she'd have the house to herself. And since Riley knew about it, he also knew she'd be alone. She'd been thinking about the pros and cons of inviting him over when the dump truck blew the side of her car apart.

"You were in a car accident, Mom. You're hurt, and the doctor said you're probably going to feel worse tomorrow."

Right. Because of her *age*.

"What kind of son would I be if I just dumped you off and went camping for a long weekend?"

Laura knew she wouldn't win this battle by just

bumping heads with him. When it came to her, Lane was going to do what he thought was right, even if she told him he didn't need to. After his father died, Lane's rigid determination to do the right thing for Laura—even when she told him she was alright—had come between him and Evie, costing him his marriage. Now that Lane and Evie had found their way back to each other, Laura wasn't going to let him make that mistake again, even if it was just a camping trip Evie had been looking forward to.

"Honey, I have a headache. Some aches and pains. All I want to do is sit in my chair and relax for a couple of days, but I can't turn off being Mom and Nana."

"And Becca's pretty loud," he said, and she was relieved he was catching on.

"She's supposed to be loud at six months. She's finding her voice and learning how to use it, but yes. She's very loud. And considering how long they're taking to discharge me, I probably *do* have time to list all the people who will be checking on me and trying to hover, but I'll just abbreviate it to Ellen and Mallory. And Molly, of course. And *her* mother."

Lane held up his hand. "You don't have to list half the town. I get it."

"The campground is less than two hours away, and Mallory said it has a good cell signal. You can check on me, and you know if there's even a hint of a problem, you'll have people stacked up in your call waiting trying to reach you."

"I don't know."

He was looking around at all the medical equipment, tension clear in his shoulders, and Laura knew being in the ER with her was keeping him on edge. "Wait until we get home before you talk to Evie about it."

She knew once she was in her chair, with the TV remote in her hand and her phone being blown up by friends checking on her, he would relax.

She hoped.

An hour later, when they pulled into the driveway, Laura was relieved to see that Evie's Jeep was the only vehicle there. She'd been in an ongoing group text exchange with the Sutton women since arriving at the hospital, and she'd told them repeatedly she was fine and just wanted to go to bed. The fact they'd listened to her was a pleasant surprise, though she knew she'd get a few more messages and possibly a phone call from Ellen before the evening was over.

And she wondered if anybody had told Riley.

The camper was gone when Riley pulled Case's truck into the equipment parking area after a *very* long day. It was the first thing he noticed because he was pleasantly surprised it was gone. Its absence meant Lane and his wife had gone on their camping trip, and *that* had to mean Laura was okay.

He hoped.

One thing he did know was that there was no way he'd just get out of Case's truck and into his and go home. Once the other guys had stowed their equipment and headed out, he pulled out his phone and sent her a text.

I have a check, but I can hold it until Monday if you're not up to it.

The response came pretty quickly, which he thought was a good sign.

I don't think you really have a check, but I wouldn't mind some company.

He laughed, shaking his head as he walked toward the house. He didn't have a check, and he'd known he'd have to confess that once he was inside, but she'd seen through it. He hadn't had the guts to just ask her if he could come in.

Laura was in the living room, in one of the two recliners with a lamp on instead of the brighter overhead light. He sat on the edge of the other recliner, looking her over. She didn't look bad, considering. Better than he'd expected, and some of the tension he'd been carrying all afternoon eased from his muscles.

"I wanted to text you, but I didn't know… I wasn't sure if you'd have your phone or not. And if Lane had it, he'd wonder why I sent the text to you and not to him."

"I didn't realize you knew about the accident or I would have told you I was okay. I escaped with a very mild concussion and some burns on my arms from the airbag. The seat belt was *very* enthusiastic about locking me in, so that didn't feel great. Some aches and pains. That's it."

"I was with them when Lane got the call. That's why I have Case's truck."

"Oh." She frowned. "That makes sense. I think my brain registered hearing Case's truck—I recognize most of them by the sound—but I didn't think about why Case would be here."

"There's that whole concussion thing," he pointed out.

"Very *mild* concussion," she countered.

He sat back in the recliner, slightly sideways so he could see her. Now that he'd seen with his own eyes that she was okay, he could finally relax. "I'm so glad you weren't hurt worse."

"Lane said my car will be totaled."

He could hear the sorrow in her voice, so he didn't let himself say that the car didn't matter at all as long as she wasn't seriously injured. "I'm sorry. It was a good car. I didn't spend a lot of time in it, but I really enjoyed our dinner in it. And it had good cup holders."

He was surprised when she made a sound that was a mixture of a laugh and a sob. "It had perfect cup holders."

"My sister's husband has a cousin who sells cars— one of those places with huge used-car lots. Once the insurance gets sorted, I can take you down and we can look at every single car until you find one with cup holders you like."

"I know from riding with other people that cup holders that fit my tumbler just right aren't easy to find."

"Bring your tumbler with you. I mean it. Every single vehicle on the lot until we find one."

She smiled, her eyes warm, as she turned in her recliner and rested her head against it so they were facing each other. "Thank you."

"For what?"

"For caring about my cup holders."

"You care about them, so I care about them, too. And I don't know what everybody's situation is with vehicles, but if you need it, you can take my truck until everything gets sorted. I have my bike."

"What if it's raining?"

"Then I'll have an excuse to ask you for a ride. I've heard you take kisses in payment."

When her bottom lip trembled and her eyes glistened with tears, he was afraid he'd said the wrong thing, but then she smiled. "I've missed you."

"I've missed you, too. I have to be honest—I tried not to. I thought maybe it would be easier for both of us if… You know, before we spend a *lot* more time together." He winced. "I don't know if that came out right."

"I know what you mean. But it wasn't easier."

"No." But he didn't want to have a deep conversation while she was still nursing a fresh concussion, no matter how mild it was. "Have you eaten?"

"Ellen left about ten minutes before I heard the trucks pull in. In addition to a casserole and half a lasagna she stress baked, she brought me some very bland soup and crackers in case my stomach is upset."

"Is it?"

"Not really. I honestly think the headache is more from the stress of the day than a concussion. Mostly my body's sore." She rolled her eyes. "And according to my doctor, I'll be more sore tomorrow, thanks to my *age*."

He tried not to laugh. He didn't succeed, but at least he tried. "I'm sorry. You know I love your age, but that face you made when you said it."

"So I'm resting so my decrepit body can heal," she said, trying not to smile.

"I haven't had my hands on as much of it as I'd like, but I do know it's not decrepit." She blushed, and that made him worry about her heart rate, so he changed the subject. "You're not watching TV?"

"No. There was nothing on worth the flickering lights and sound. I've been trying to read because books comfort me, but focusing my eyes on the page makes the headache worse. The library doesn't have an audiobook version that I can listen to. They have others, but I hate reading two books at the same time, which means I won't go back to this one and I won't know who killed her husband."

"Ah," he said, leaning toward the end table between the two chairs to pick up the paperback with the blurry image of a woman's face on the cover. "The dead-husband genre."

"It's my favorite," she said with a smile that probably would have worried him if he was her husband.

"Tell you what. You let me dip into that stress-baked lasagna and then I'll read to you."

Chapter Nine

*Don't forget that the next meeting of the Books
& Brews book club is this coming Wednesday at
Sutton's Place Brewery & Tavern! At the end of
the evening, you can vote on the three finalists
for next month's read. Mr. Avery tells us he tried
to open it up to suggestions, but he ended up with
fourteen suggestions for fourteen different books.
Voting on three finalists chosen by a secret committee (we think it's Mr. Avery, Molly Cyrs and
Irish Sutton, but we can't confirm) is how it will
be going forward. Get to reading, everybody!*
—Stonefield Gazette *Facebook Page*

If anybody had ever asked Laura to make a list of
all the things she found sexy in a man, it probably

would have had all the typical things. The way they smelled—before they worked all day in the sun. Deep voices whispering sexy things. Strong forearms. Definitely the forearms. The way the hard lines of their faces softened when they were asleep. A strong, calloused hand cupping the back of her neck during a long kiss.

It had never occurred to her that a man reading a thriller aloud to her would not only make the list, but shoot straight to the top.

Riley read in a deep, even tone. He captured the inflection of the passages without being overly dramatic, and he didn't rush. With the lights off, except the reading lamp he was using, and her recliner kicked back, her headache was slowly fading away.

She could listen to him read for hours.

And she had been. He'd been reading to her for over two hours, though he'd paused once when Ellen had called to check on her. And he'd gone outside when her phone had signaled an incoming video chat from Lane. She'd appreciated that he didn't want Lane asking questions about why he was there with her so late, but it had still been awkward. But then he'd resumed reading and the subtle tension had faded.

She hadn't realized she'd nodded off until Riley tugging her blanket down over her feet woke her. He smiled when her eyes opened, and she gave him a smile in return.

"I was trying not to wake you," he said softly.

"If you're sure you're okay, I'll go home so you can go to bed."

Laura wanted to ask him to stay with her. The question echoed around in her mind, but she didn't give voice to it. She was okay as far as not needing a caretaker, but the aches and pains were no joke. If and when—and it was leaning more and more toward *when*—she and Riley made love, she wanted to enjoy every second of it.

"I'm okay," she said.

"Make sure you take your cell phone with you to bed," he said. "And I know there's a whole list of people above me on the list you'll reach out to if you need anything, but I'll have my phone next to my bed. I put you in my Favorites list, so even if I accidentally put it in Do Not Disturb, which I'm known to do, you can get through. If there's anything at all I can do, you call me."

"I'm in your Favorites?" She couldn't help smiling at that.

"You are definitely in my Favorites." Then he leaned down and kissed her forehead. "Good night, Laura."

The sigh of resignation escaped before she could stop it. "Good night."

He didn't want to leave. It was written all over his face, and she knew if she asked him to stay with her, even though there would be *no* making out, he would. But she couldn't bring herself to ask him to do that. She didn't trust herself not to try to lure him into her bedroom. He'd say no because it would be the right thing to do. That would be painful for both of them, so she watched him walk out the door instead. After a few minutes, she heard his truck start—he'd parked it down by the garage—and then drive away.

By Sunday afternoon, Laura was heartily sick of people asking her if she was okay. By phone. By text message. By video chat. Ellen, Mallory, Gwen and Amanda had all been to the house. Even Case had made a brief appearance in her living room, probably as a favor to Lane.

It was an ongoing thing through the weekend, except for when the sun went down. Riley had turned up after supper last night and read to her, just as he had Friday night. And once again, when she got drowsy, he'd kissed her forehead and said good-night.

If he came over again tonight, it would be anytime. She paced the kitchen, wiping down a counter that was already clean and trying not to look out the window for the umpteenth time.

When she finally heard the familiar sound of his truck turning into the lower driveway, she inhaled deeply and allowed herself a silly moment of hugging herself and grinning like a girl on prom night.

By the time his footsteps crossed the porch, though, she'd regained her composure, and she met him at the door with a more reasonable smile. "I wasn't sure you'd come over tonight. Even Lane has slowed down as far as checking on me."

"We're pretty close to the end of that book, and we disagree on whodunit, so I've got to keep reading."

She walked toward her recliner, but didn't sit yet. "Did you already eat? I swear, I don't know what Ellen and Amanda were thinking. Even if Lane and Evie were home, they brought too much food."

"I did eat. But I'm pretty shameless, so if you want to send some home with me, I won't say no."

She laughed and dropped into her chair. "Don't let me forget to pack you some, then. I'd hate to throw it away."

"How are you feeling?" he asked as he picked up the book and turned on the reading lamp before sitting in the other recliner.

"Much better, I think. The doctor was right about yesterday. I was *very* sore, but some warm soaks in the tub and painkillers helped. And today the aches and pains are a lot less noticeable."

"Well, don't overdo it," he said, giving her a stern look that made her laugh.

Then he opened the book to the yarn store receipt she'd been using as a bookmark and started to read.

They were getting close to the end, she thought as she settled in to listen to his voice in the dim light. They were close to the end of the book. And close to the end of Lane and Evie's camping trip. These evenings with Riley had become her favorite part of the day, and she was about to lose them.

Not that she'd be lonely. She missed Becca, and there was nothing like having a baby in the house to keep things lively. And Lane and Evie were good company, to say nothing of Ellen and the various knitting and gardening and book clubs they belonged to.

But this quiet time with Riley was something special that filled a void she hadn't even recognized was present until he came into her life. Not only did she love his reading voice, but she loved the back-and-forth they had when he'd stop at the end of each chapter and they'd offer theories on what was going on with the suspense plot. It was especially fun that they had two different theories.

"Are you still listening?" he asked in a teasing voice.

She opened her eyes and nodded, even though she might have missed a little bit of the last couple of pages. "Just resting my eyes."

He snorted. "My dad says that right before he starts snoring."

"I was *mostly* listening," she confessed, though she wasn't going to admit she hadn't been dozing, but had been thinking about how much she was going to miss him reading to her. "But tomorrow's a workday. You can't stay up late."

"It's a workday for me, but I hope you won't be working tomorrow."

She laughed. "What I do isn't quite as strenuous as what you do."

"Maybe not physically, but sitting all day is hard on the body, and anybody who thinks customer service and accounting aren't strenuous has never done them." He shook his head. "I know you won't stay out of your office, but I hope you'll stick to easy stuff and leave the hard stuff. I know Evie helps you out in the office, and she'll be well rested and able to handle catching up when she gets back."

"Oh, I'm sure camping with a six-month-old baby is all kinds of restful." She laughed. "But I'll take it easy tomorrow."

She watched him flip through the pages left after the receipt. "I hope we'll be able to finish it tomorrow night."

"Maybe come over a little earlier and we'll have supper together," she said. "I'll tell everybody to leave me alone so I can enjoy my last night of peace and quiet."

"It's a date," he said, and the way his gaze held hers told her it wasn't just an expression. It would be a real date, even though they wouldn't leave her house.

He was about to speak when her cell phone rang, and Laura resisted the urge to chuck it against the wall so hard it would never interrupt her and Riley again. Instead, she looked at the name on the screen.

"It's Ellen," she said.

"You should take that." Before she could tell him no—that she'd call Ellen back tomorrow—he'd kissed her forehead again and headed for the door. "I'll see you tomorrow after work."

Laura took a second to get the urge to curse a lot under control before accepting the call from Ellen. Her friend had been talking to Amanda about the missing gazebo budget situation, and they had some thoughts she wanted to share.

She tried to pay attention, but she didn't really care about whether or not the gazebo got painted. She was too busy wishing the phone hadn't rung and gotten her another forehead kiss.

It was a sweet gesture—more tender than she'd ever been accustomed to—but she would rather have gotten a real kiss tonight. One that left her breathless and aching for more.

Tomorrow night, she vowed while Ellen ranted about the condition of the town landmark. Tomorrow night Riley was going to kiss her the way she yearned to be kissed.

"Take your shirt off." As she said the words, Laura was beckoning with her fingers.

Riley grinned, appreciating the upturn in what hadn't been a great Monday. "Now, that's how a man likes to be greeted after a long day of work."

She looked confused for a few seconds, and then she laughed. "Don't get your hopes up, Riley. You got stung today, and I want to make sure you're okay."

He *was* okay, but he wasn't going to turn down an opportunity to have her hands on his naked skin. He tugged the hem of his T-shirt free from his jeans and then pulled it over his head.

Her gaze was anything but clinical as it raked over his chest, and he shivered as though the look was a physical caress. Then she cleared her throat and her gaze returned to his face.

"Where are they?"

He shrugged. "Back of my shoulder, but I promise I'm fine. It's not a big deal, Laura."

She put her hands on her hips and nodded toward her desk chair. "I'll be the judge of that. Sit."

He sat. And even though he knew she was going to touch him, nothing could have prepared him for the warmth of her hands skimming across his back. Closing his eyes, he let her run her fingertips over his skin and ignored the fact she wasn't doing it for pleasure.

It had been his own fault—he hadn't seen the hive—and the hornets had not taken kindly to the vibration of his chain saw biting through the tree limb. When they'd had enough, he'd been thirty feet in the air, and all he could do was crouch in the bucket and listen to the murderously angry insects ping against his safety helmet. It had been years since he'd been stung on the job, but he considered himself lucky to have gotten away with one sting on his right shoulder and three on his left. They didn't feel great when the fabric of his shirt stretched across them, but it could have been worse.

He didn't wince when she used her fingernail to ensure there were no stingers left in the skin. He knew there weren't. He'd checked when it happened, and again when he'd run home to take a speed record-setting shower before driving back and parking his truck beside the garage. And he didn't argue when she told him to sit right there and she'd be right back.

Alone, he closed his eyes for a few seconds and let his thoughts wander to where they'd been all day. Lane and Evie would be returning tomorrow, probably by early afternoon. This was the last night he and Laura would be alone in this house, and he wondered if she was as aware of that fact as he was.

And if so, what were they going to do about it? With every passing day, he grew more convinced Laura was worth risking everything for, but it wasn't easy to make that first move—to take her in his arms and straight past the point of no return.

He'd gone to the interview with Lane and Case in a position of power. They'd wanted him more than he'd needed them, and that gave him the upper hand. He hadn't loved his previous job, but it had paid well enough and he only had to jump ship if he wanted to. And Lane had all but told him the job was his and the interview was a formality. Riley's reputation and safety record had preceded him, and he'd crossed paths with them a few times over the years, so they weren't total strangers.

But now the power dynamic had shifted a little. If Lane fired him, he'd either have to go back to his former employer with hat in hand, or go knocking on other doors. He wouldn't have any trouble finding work, but he'd lose the advantage. He'd probably take a pay cut and have to start on a lower rung of a company's ladder. And, as an added bonus, he'd be doing it all from a funeral home in a middle-of-nowhere town.

The photo on the desk caught his attention—the one of her and her husband, laughing with a very young Lane and Evie—and he leaned forward to study it. Laura looked so happy in the picture, and maybe he was giving himself too much credit, but he thought she looked that happy when she was with him.

When he heard Laura's footsteps approaching, he leaned back in her chair, though he didn't turn it to face her.

"This might sting a bit," she said. "And it'll be cold."

He nodded and sat still while she applied an ointment of some sort to each of the stings.

"Shane said it was a big nest and you're lucky it wasn't worse."

"Shane's exaggerating a little bit. If it was a big nest, I would have seen it." He should have seen it, anyway, but he'd started thinking about this being Laura's last Lane-free night as soon as he opened his eyes that morning, and he might have been a little distracted. He was lucky he'd gotten away with a few bee stings. "And when did you talk to Shane?"

"You were still up in the bucket when he called me. I told him when he started here that any injuries have to be reported to me as soon as they happen, and that boy follows directions to the letter. Then he called me back a few minutes later to tell me you'd cursed a lot and put some ice on them for maybe thirty seconds, and you were already back in the bucket."

He nodded, but didn't say anything because he wanted *her* to keep talking. As she became lost in what she was saying, her hands had started roaming over his shoulders, and he really liked that. And when her thumb pressed circles into the base of his neck, he dropped his head slightly to give her more access, but he bit back the moan that might have alerted her to what she was doing.

Then her hands froze, and he knew she'd become aware of it, anyway. Before she could pull away, he covered her hands with his, pressing their warmth to his skin. There was a slight tremble in the touch, but he honestly couldn't say if it was her or him.

She slid her hands over his chest for a regrettably short time, and then pulled them free. "I put one of Ellen's casseroles in the oven a little while ago. It should be ready now."

He was starving, but not for casserole. He craved more of her touch, but he nodded and pushed himself to his feet. He'd take his cues from her, and her cue had been pulling away.

"Lane and Evie will be home tomorrow," she said once they were seated at the table.

If there was one thing Riley was all too aware of, it was the fact his time alone with Laura was coming to an end. "Case showed me some of the pictures Evie posted, and it looks like they're having a great time."

"Lane sounds a lot more relaxed on the phone. I wish they could stay longer, even though I miss my little Becca."

Riley wished they could stay longer, too, though for a very different reason than Lane's state of mind.

"It's been so quiet without her here," Laura continued. "Though having the house all to myself has been nice. That doesn't happen very often anymore."

"Since you kind of opened that door, I've been wondering—who moved in with who? I mean, did you move in with them or did they move in with you?"

He was afraid she'd find the question too intrusive, but she only smiled. "My husband bought this house. Lane grew up in it. When he married Evie, they rented a place of their own, but then Joe died and they moved back in. A few months later, their marriage was over and Evie left town. It's a big house, and the garage and all the equipment are here, so I guess it never made sense for Lane to pay for his own place."

"But Evie came back to town, and now they're happily married a second time, with a daughter."

"Yes." He loved the way her face lit up. "And again, it's a big house. They took over the upstairs, including a little sitting room, so everybody can have their own space. Maybe it wouldn't work for all families, but it works for us."

"But it's *your* house." He wasn't sure why he pushed that point, other than wanting to remind her she was free to do what she wanted in her own house.

But her brow furrowed, making him wonder if he'd overstepped. "Technically—*legally*, I guess— yes, the entire property belongs to me, and the tree service leases the garage and that yard space. But it was Joe's and it's meant to be Lane's, and I guess I just live here in the meantime. But in my heart, it's really Lane's."

He nodded, though he didn't fully understand what she meant. And he didn't want to talk about Lane anymore tonight. His boss would be back tomorrow and he wanted the time he had left with Laura to be about her—about *them*.

"Ellen Sutton makes a damn fine cheeseburger casserole," he said, resting his silverware on his empty plate.

"I'll tell her you said so," she said, obviously pleased by the compliment to her friend's cooking.

He wondered if she really would pass the compliment along, though. She'd said Ellen knew they'd gone to the movies, but it had been obvious the few times he'd been here when her friend called that she didn't know he'd been spending his evenings with Laura.

When he stood to carry his plate to the sink, she stopped him with a wave of her hand. "I'll clean up. We're almost to the end of the book, and I'm dying to know what happens, so you read and I'll wash."

They hadn't used many dishes, so he only got one chapter in before they moved to the living room. Instead of dimming everything but the reading light and sitting in her recliner, she sat on the couch. Not one to pass up that kind of opportunity, he settled on the couch next to her.

He opened the book and picked up reading where he'd left off, but a few pages later—just when the fictional widow was about to open a padded envelope that had been left under her windshield wiper—Laura spoke.

"Will you stay with me tonight?"

The book slipped from his fingers, losing the page, as he looked at her. Her hair was framing her face, and she looked so beautiful his heart ached. "I want to."

"But?" she prompted after a few seconds.

"I'm pretty sure if exercise is on the list of things you're not supposed to be doing with a concussion, then sex is definitely on the list." He grinned and twisted a lock of her hair around his finger. "If you're doing it right, anyway."

"It was barely a concussion. I'll call the doctor right now and put him on speakerphone. He said I'd have a headache and that *maybe* I might have a very mild concussion. And for your information, he didn't give me any limitations. He said I should rest for a couple of days, and then if something was too much, to stop doing it."

"If reading gives you a headache, what do you think sex is going to do?"

She laughed. "Reading gave me a headache the day of the accident."

"And you've had me reading to you this whole weekend?" he asked in mock outrage. He didn't mind. In fact, there was nothing else he'd rather be doing.

"I love listening to you read to me, so I just let you believe you needed to. I thought about going to the library to get a romance novel so you could read the sexy parts to me, but I was afraid that would only make everything worse."

He tilted his head. "Everything?"

"This…" She waved her hand between them. "The wanting you and not being able to have you. Listening to you read a sex scene to me was *not* going to help with that."

His entire body ached with the strain of not hauling her onto his lap and kissing her senseless. "You can have me anytime you want. The only person stopping you is you."

"It's complicated. You know why. But tonight I don't care."

"Tomorrow you'll care, though. And I know all the reasons you *think* it's complicated. Personally, I think it's our business what we do."

She sighed and pulled away just enough so her hair fell free of his fingers. "I don't think Lane would fire you. He's not petty like that. But I can't guarantee he won't be a jerk about it, and nobody wants to stay in a hostile work environment."

"It's a risk I'm willing to take." He meant every word of it. "Tell me something, and be honest about it. If nobody else was involved—if I didn't work for the tree service and nobody in Stonefield knew me— what would you want?"

Her mouth curved into a smile. "You'd be naked in my bed right now. And it wouldn't be the first time, either."

For a few seconds, Riley was sure he'd burst into flames, because it certainly felt like he had. "You're killing me, Laura."

"Hey, the only person stopping you is you."

He chuckled, not surprised she'd turned his words around on him. "You're talking about gossip. I'm talking about your actual, physical health."

"Don't you think the fact we each keep coming up with reasons why it's a bad idea for the other person is a sign it's a bad idea?"

He captured her hair between his fingers again because he liked the feel of it. "I think it means I care about you and don't want you to overdo it after your accident, and you care about me and don't want me to get jammed up with my boss."

"Are you saying you won't stay with me tonight?"

He slowly shook his head. "That's not what I'm saying. I don't think it's even possible for me to say that."

Her gaze dropped to his mouth, and she inhaled

deeply before letting out a slow breath. "Do you want to read another chapter first?"

With a growl, he tossed the book onto the coffee table and reached for her. Fisting his hand in her hair, he kissed her the way he'd been aching to kiss her every night.

Chapter Ten

We promised you the results from our pizza poll, and nobody who's lived in Stonefield for any length of time will be surprised by the results. Forty-three percent of you think a pizza with no sauce is still a pizza. And 43 percent of you believe a pizza with no sauce is just a round cheesy bread. (Fourteen percent of you don't care, but don't like being left out of polls.) It's a tie, so the debate will rage on. Knowing this town, probably for generations.
     —Stonefield Gazette *Facebook Page*

Laura did something she hadn't done since her husband died—she took a man by the hand and led him into her bedroom. She'd spent the occasional night elsewhere over the last decade or so, but had never invited anybody into *her* bed.

She wanted Riley there. She wanted him naked on her favorite mauve sheets with the ridiculously high thread count. She wanted his head on her pillow and his hands on her body. And tonight, she was going to have him.

Laura was about to turn and face him when he let go of her hand and slid his arms around her waist. He pulled her close, so her back was to his chest, and then he nuzzled her hair out of the way so he could kiss the side of her neck.

She leaned back, tilting her head and lifting her hair out of the way so he was free to kiss the sensitive flesh below her ear and work his way around to the nape of her neck. She shivered under the heat of his mouth, and the vibration of his chuckle against her skin tickled.

His hands roamed over her body, their bodies swaying together slightly, as if they were dancing. Then he slowly turned her to face him. He kissed her hard, his hand fisted in her hair, and then he kissed his way down her jaw and her neck, until she threw her head back so he could dip his tongue into the hollow of her throat.

When his hands slid under her shirt, lifting it over her head, she had a moment of gratitude it was *mostly* dark. She'd expected to be more self-conscious about her body because, though she was in fairly good shape, it was still a forty-eight-year-old body. Riley didn't seem to mind, though, and she wasn't about to argue with him.

"You are so freaking beautiful," he said as he cupped her breasts, and she felt the warmth of his hands through the fabric of her bra. She could see the way he looked at her—and she believed him.

He kissed her as his thumbs ran across her nipples, making her shiver. And then he was kissing his way down her neck, and she wanted his clothes off of him. He took the hint when she started fumbling with the fly of his jeans, and within what seemed like seconds, every inch of his work-hardened body was visible. She moaned slightly, taking in the sight of him, and he grinned as he started pushing her pants down her hips.

Laura thought she'd step out of them, but Riley lifted her and set her on the bed. Then he leaned over her, kissing her again, before tugging the rest of her clothes off and tossing them aside.

She had a moment, when he was standing over her and devouring her with his gaze, when she was tempted to hide herself—the soft stomach and the breasts that didn't look as good without the support of her bra—but the sound of appreciation he made changed her mind.

When he ran his hands up the insides of her thighs and pushed them apart, she sucked in a breath. Then his mouth was on her, and she balled the bedcovers in her fists as delicious sensations shot through her body.

Oh, he was *very* good at that.

Only when she squirmed and hit the top of his shoulder with the heel of her hand did he stop the relentless, teasing licking and sucking. He nipped at the soft skin of her thigh and then kissed his way up her body.

She reached between their bodies, taking him in her hand, and he sucked in a ragged breath. "Oh, no, you don't. You're recuperating, so I'm doing all the work."

Riley must have had a condom in his pocket, because there was one on the nightstand that hadn't been there before. Laura's body quivered in anticipation as he rolled it on and settled himself between her thighs.

He was gentle when he guided himself into her, but she could see how much it was costing him by the way his body trembled slightly. With each slow thrust, she took more of him, and she skimmed her nails up his back.

Their gazes locked and the heat she saw there made her shiver.

"I've wanted this since the first time I walked into that office," he said in a husky voice.

"Me, too," she admitted in barely more than a whisper.

"I've thought about it every night since then." She nodded, and then gasped when he pushed harder into her. "You feel even better than I imagined."

Then his mouth was on hers as his hips rocked,

driving into her. The sweet friction made her whimper, and she grabbed his ass, urging him faster.

"Laura," he groaned, and it was enough.

The orgasm hit hard, and her back arched off the bed as she dug her fingernails into his skin. He thrust harder and faster, and then his body shook as he came.

When he collapsed on top of her, she wrapped her arms around him as he buried his face in her hair. Then she hooked her legs around his so he couldn't move. She wasn't ready to let him go yet.

"I wanted you so bad," he said, his hot breath tickling her ear. "Next time I'm going to take my time."

She stroked his hair. "Next time?"

"I don't want you overdoing it, so we need to make sure your head doesn't hurt." Then he chuckled. "And, as you may have heard, I'm not as young as I look. I'll need a minute."

She laughed and then let him go so he could dispose of the condom. Stretching, she savored the delicious feeling of a body well satisfied—despite some lingering soreness from the accident—and then pulled down the covers so they could snuggle properly.

Yes, they were definitely going to take their time the next time. And maybe the time after that.

Riley woke with a start, Laura's curse breaking into a dream he already couldn't remember.

Not the way a man liked to wake up after a long

night of lovemaking. He blinked against the morning light streaming through the window as she threw
back the covers, and it took a few seconds for his
brain to catch up with what was going on.

Bright morning light. Laura rushing to pull on
clothes. The sound of a truck pulling into the lower
driveway.

Echoing *her* curse with one of his own, he slid
out of bed and started pulling on the clothes he'd
shed last night. The guys were showing up for work,
and here he was, naked in the bedroom of the boss's
mom. Not that he regretted it. He didn't—not a single
second. But he'd rather not get caught.

"They'll just assume you parked down there and
then walked up because you needed something from
the office," she was saying. "You've done it before,
and it's a perfectly sensible reason for you to be in
my house at this hour."

"Don't you have an alarm?" he asked as he tucked
his T-shirt into his jeans. Doing the walk of shame
was one thing. Doing an entire workday of shame
wasn't something he'd ever done before. Luckily, he'd
put on clean clothes after his shower before coming
over last night, so at least it wouldn't be obvious to
the guys.

"I haven't bothered to use one for a long time.
I'm usually up early, and if I don't wake up on my
own, Becca fixes that. Don't *you* have an alarm on
your phone? Isn't that what most people use now?"

"I don't know what most people use, but I have an

actual alarm clock in my room because I charge my phone in the living room so I can't watch funny videos past my bedtime." He scrubbed his hands through his hair, trying to wake up. "And, trust me, alarm clocks were the last thing on my mind last night."

Their eyes met and Laura's hands stilled on her shirt buttons. For a few seconds, the temptation was there—maybe they could call in sick and go back to bed for a couple of hours.

He could do a *lot* with a couple of hours.

But his truck was in the pit and the guys would wonder why. And if Laura said she didn't feel well, Case wasn't going to just shrug it off and head out to the job. Hell, he'd probably call Lane and Ellen and everybody else.

Then Laura looked away, breaking the connection as she finished buttoning the shirt. "There are wrapped toothbrushes in the middle drawer in my bathroom—the kind the dentist gives out—but hurry up before somebody comes up here looking for you."

When he was finished in her bathroom, the bedroom was empty. He found her in the kitchen, where she was putting the lid on a travel mug with the Perkin' Up Café logo embossed on it. Once it was tight, she held it out to him.

"Thanks," he said, taking a sip of the desperately needed coffee even though it burned his mouth.

"There's no time for breakfast," she said, obviously upset as she led the way to her office. Once he'd followed her in, she visibly relaxed. Now they were at least where people would expect to find them. Hopefully those people wouldn't notice she looked as if she'd just fallen out of bed after a very thorough tumble between the sheets.

"I keep granola bars in the truck. I'll have a couple of them and I'll be fine."

"You can't work all day on a couple of granola bars. And you don't have time before the first job to grab anything on the way."

"But I have time between them to have an early lunch. I promise I'll be fine."

She blew out a breath, and then she noticed that breath moved some strands that she'd missed when twisting her hair into a hasty knot. After running her hand over her head, she gave him a look that told him she'd just realized she wasn't nearly as put together as she'd hoped she was.

And then she laughed, and the relief made him laugh along with her. He hadn't wanted to leave her so obviously agitated, and her laughter eased the tension that had been between them since she woke and realized they'd overslept.

"I thought we'd wake up and have a nice breakfast together," she said, giving him a regretful smile, though amusement still sparkled in her eyes.

"I thought we'd wake up and skip breakfast so we could make love again," he said, and she laughed again. "I put those extra granola bars in my truck, just in case."

After going still for a few seconds, as if listen-

ing for footsteps, she grabbed the front of his T-shirt
and pulled him in for a kiss. It was fast and hard,
and over before he had a chance to make it into the
kind of kiss he would have liked to leave her with.

Then she smoothed his shirt and gave him a once-
over before nodding. "You should go, before they
come looking for you. You look fine, but I get the
feeling I might not."

He started to walk away, but turned back in the
doorway. "You look gorgeous. Even with your shirt
buttoned wrong."

Case was halfway across the yard when Riley
stepped out onto the porch and pulled the door closed
behind him. He'd obviously been looking for him,
because he stopped walking and waited rather than
continuing to the house.

"Laura had a couple of questions about the job
slip I turned in Friday," he said, surprised and a little
dismayed by how easily the lie fell out of his mouth.

"No problem. We've got to head out, though.
Chester's big into punctuality. He doesn't have cable
because they wouldn't give him better than a four-
hour window and he told them never mind."

Riley laughed, not sure if that was a true story,
or if Case had made it a little more colorful to make
a point. The laughter died quickly, though, when an
image of Case walking in and finding him coming
out of Laura's bedroom popped into his head. If the
truck hadn't woken Laura, that was probably what
would have happened. Case would have looked for

them in the office and, not finding them, probably would have called for her. Short of going out the window, there would have been no way for Riley to get out of the bedroom without being seen.

He wondered if Laura would have made him climb out the window and snorted.

"You okay?" Case asked as they reached the truck.

"What? Oh, yeah. I was just thinking about not having cable because they wouldn't promise to show up at one twenty on the dot." Again with the easy lie.

He bent and greeted Boomer enthusiastically. Case was definitely the dog's favorite human, but he genuinely seemed to adore everybody he met, and Riley loved that about him. If he could somehow guarantee he'd get a dog as good as Boomer, he'd get one in a heartbeat.

"Are you sure you're okay?" Case asked again when they were on the road. "You seem a little off."

"I forgot to turn my alarm on and overslept." Finally, a truth. It didn't last long, though. "I woke up late, and I had a text message from Laura asking me to go up and see her before we left, so I didn't have time for breakfast. That's why I'm eating this granola bar, which, no matter how hard I try, does not taste like a bacon-and-cheese omelet."

"How's Aunt Laura doing, anyway?"

Riley winced. Sometimes, with the guys, it was easy to forget it was messy, and then a *mom* or an *aunt* would get tossed out and he'd remember again.

"She seems really good. Maybe a little soreness, but she said no headaches or anything."

"I saw the car, and she got lucky. I'm glad she wasn't hurt badly."

Riley's stomach knotted at the thought of what could have happened. "Me, too."

"She must be missing Becca, though," Case continued. "I know Ellen is."

"Best friends sharing a granddaughter is pretty cool."

"It is. When David passed away, we all worried about Ellen. Having all of her daughters home definitely helped, but I think it was her friendship with Laura that really got her through it. They do almost everything together, and they probably always will."

The words sent a pang of guilt through Riley, even though he knew he hadn't done anything wrong. But not wanting to take Laura's time away from Ellen was yet another thread in the tangled web he'd woven for himself.

Case was quiet for a few moments, and then he cleared his throat. "I heard your truck was here in the evenings, and the light was on in the garage."

Was it Riley's guilty conscience, or was there a slight edge to the other man's tone? "I had stuff to do to keep me busy, and it kept me close in case Laura needed something from the store or…whatever."

"I appreciate you being around extra in case Laura needed anything." He cast a sideways glance in Riley's direction. "When I told Lane, he definitely appreciated it, too."

Riley nodded, unable to say anything past the lump in his throat. He'd left the light on deliberately in the evenings just in case nosy passersby had spotted his truck beside the garage and said something. Obviously the subterfuge had paid off, but he hated that he'd done it.

They rolled up to a stop sign, and through the corner of his eye, he saw Case watching him. There was something curious—questioning?—in the look, and Riley couldn't bring himself to meet the man's eyes.

Instead, he held up the second granola bar, still in the wrapper. His appetite was gone. "Want a granola bar?"

Chapter Eleven

A news item offered without editorial comment: Earlier today, somebody called the Stonefield Police Department to report that the Stonefield Police Department was stealing donations from the fire department's Badges For Backpacks donation drop-off box. Fire Chief Nelson had no comment. Police Chief Bordeaux offered the following: "FD probably hid the stuff to drum up sympathy donations."

—Stonefield Gazette *Facebook Page*

Laura didn't want the morning-after fiasco to be how things stood between her and Riley. They'd exchanged a few text messages, but they hadn't told her much about what he was thinking. Based on the time sent, the first had come while he was finally eating breakfast.

I'm sorry this morning was chaotic.

It felt impersonal, but she'd realized he might have done that deliberately, in case somebody else picked up her phone. She didn't like it, but she understood it.

Me too. I'm sorry I panicked.

I get it. And it is what it is.

She ran the last sentence through her mind, trying different inflections and tones, but she couldn't find a way to translate that as *I can't wait to see you again*, and that bothered her. The morning hadn't been good, but the night together had been amazing. She wanted more, and when they'd parted ways, she'd gotten the impression he did, too. But maybe with some distance from her, he'd realized how ridiculous their situation was.

He sent the next text in the late afternoon, while she had a lapful of exhausted baby, and Lane and Evie were streaming their vacation photos to the TV screen. They'd taken an astonishing number for a long weekend.

Did you finish the book?

She'd typed out a response one-handed, not wanting to drop Becca. And also, she might have used the baby as a shield so Lane and Evie wouldn't see her texting and know her attention had wandered away from the eighty-ninth picture of Becca in the babies' splash pool.

I haven't had time. And I don't want to finish it without you. It's not the same.

When he didn't respond, she told herself that was okay. It happened a lot when the guys were working, and hopefully he'd text her back the next time he had a minute.

It turned out to be hours. Hours when she didn't know if he had no interest in "reading" with her again or if he was busy. Hours when she tried to focus on being happy her family was home and not resenting them for keeping her from having an evening with Riley to look forward to.

Her phone chimed an hour after they'd finished eating supper, and when she saw it was from him, her pulse quickened. She read the words twice, hope making itself known by taking her breath away.

Can you come down to the garage? Tell them I had mentioned going shopping earlier and you asked me to grab you some cookies.

Did you actually bring me cookies?

Of course. I'm good at lying, I guess.

Ouch. He didn't seem like the kind of guy who liked being dishonest, and she didn't love it, either. But they'd both known when she asked him to stay that it would be complicated. Neither of them had kept quiet about their reservations.

I'll be right down.

Lane and Evie were in the living room, watching an episode of a show they'd missed while camping. Becca was asleep on Lane's chest, so she kept her voice low and tried to sound as casual as possible.

"I'm going down to the garage for a few minutes. Riley had said he was going to the market earlier, so I asked him to grab me some cookies."

"Do you want me to go get them?" Lane asked, as she'd known he would.

"You have a baby sleeping on you," she pointed out. "And I was cooped up in the house all weekend. It's not a long walk, but a little fresh air will do me good."

Lane nodded and turned his attention back to the show, but Evie gave her a questioning look. Laura had no idea what her expression did, but Evie grinned and then mouthed silent words. *I'll keep him here.*

There was nothing she could say to that, so she turned away. Her sweater was hung by the back door, and she pulled it on before stepping outside. It was unseasonably chilly tonight, thanks to a cool breeze.

When she slipped through the side door, Riley was there. He pulled her inside and kicked the door closed, before moving them away from the door's windowpanes. Then he kissed her so thoroughly, all she could do was moan and relax her body against his.

"I missed you," he mumbled against her lips.

"I missed you, too."

"I wish I'd come up with a better excuse. It only takes a second to grab a package of cookies."

"Yes, but I love to talk. It's not unusual for things to take me twice as long as they should because I'm yapping."

"Then I have time to kiss you again."

She didn't bother answering because it would take precious seconds. Instead, she wrapped her arms around his neck and hauled his mouth back to hers. His fingertips bit into her waist, and she groaned when he pulled her hard against his body.

"I wish we had more time," he whispered.

"Me, too. Soon. I'll figure it out."

"Maybe *you* should borrow Irish's camper and run away for a long weekend."

She laughed, though it sounded perfect. "I'd never get out of town without Ellen."

"Okay, you should probably go before we end up naked on the garage floor." With a reluctant sigh, Riley reached into the bag set on a workbench and then handed her a package of cookies. "Don't forget these."

She took the cookies and held them to her chest. "Will I see you tomorrow?"

"I hope so. I'll try."

The frustration she felt at this sneaking around was mirrored on his face, and she sighed. There was nothing else to do but go back to the house and wish he was there with her. "Thank you for the cookies."

He nodded, and she realized by the shadow that crossed his eyes that was the wrong thing to say. He hadn't bought them for her as a treat. He'd bought them to cover the lie they had to tell to be alone for a few minutes.

She ate two of them in the kitchen, and then she said good-night to Lane and Evie and went to her room. The bed was still unmade. She hadn't been able to bring herself to smooth the evidence of Riley's body out of her sheets. Now she slid into the place he'd slept last night, even though it was the wrong side of the bed, just because she wanted to feel him close to her.

Riley was exhausted. He'd worked hard today, as if he was punishing himself, and his body ached. And maybe it was his imagination, but it sure seemed like Case had given him a few suspicious looks over the course of the day.

He was *not* cut out for sneaking around, that was for damn sure. And the worst part was, he couldn't even get a little sympathy or a nice back rub from his girlfriend because nobody could know that was what Laura was to him—at least in his mind, anyway.

After dumping some ice in his largest tumbler and filling it with water, he sank onto his couch with a sigh. Maybe there was something mindless on TV that would lull him into a nap. Or something action-packed that might distract him from thinking about Laura and the fact he couldn't have dinner with her tonight. Or read to her. Or anything else.

Then his phone rang.

For a few seconds, he thought it was Laura and his mood instantly lifted, but then he saw the word *Mom* across a picture of the two of them together and sighed. He hadn't called her in a few days, having been wrapped up in what was happening with Laura, and she probably wasn't happy about it.

"Hi, Mom."

"Hi, honey. Are you busy?"

"Not at the moment." But just in case she was in a mood, he wanted to give himself an out. "I'm going out in a few minutes, but I can talk. How are things with you?"

"Good. Did your father tell you we're going on a cruise next spring?" she asked, and he chuckled. "I know, but he has his heart set on it, and once he showed me all the included dining options, I was sold."

"I think you'll have a great time." He could definitely see his parents on a cruise. His dad would probably buy a tropical shirt and his mom would wear a floppy hat.

"How is Stonefield? Are you meeting new people?"

"It's good. I'm actually going to go to the bar in a bit and hang out. It's a friendly town. And…" He hesitated, but he wanted to tell *somebody* about Laura. "I've met a woman I like."

His mom made a little *oh* sound, and then her happy sigh echoed down the line. "Tell me about her."

"Her name is Laura and she's amazing. I was thinking about inviting her to your birthday, if you don't mind."

"Mind? I can't wait to meet her! I don't think you've brought a girl home to meet us since you were in high school."

The *girl* made him wince, and he wondered if he should tell her more about Laura than the fact she was amazing. But if he told her everything about the situation, she might have strong feelings about it, and he didn't want to hear it. And it would also make it harder to invite Laura to meet his family. He knew his parents well enough to know they wouldn't make a scene in front of her, so he decided to wait.

He'd also belatedly realized there was a possibility Lane would find out what had been going on and Riley's world would implode before he got a chance to introduce her to them, and he probably shouldn't have said anything at all.

"How are the kids doing?" he asked, knowing talking about her grandchildren was a good distraction.

Twenty minutes later, he was totally caught up on the lives of his sisters and his nieces and nephews. He'd even managed to stay awake during the entire conversation, which had been very one-sided. But he was thankful he'd preemptively offered up an excuse to end the call. He reminded her he was on his way out and promised to call in a few days.

Then he sat in the silent apartment with its very cheery yellow walls and decided the television wasn't going to be enough of a distraction to keep him from spending the rest of the night wishing he was with Laura.

Rather than doing nothing but missing her and feeling sorry for himself, Riley forced himself to get up off the couch. He grabbed his keys and his wallet and headed for Sutton's Place. He walked because it was a nice night and the fresh air would do him good.

Plus, if he was going to drink enough beer to make him forget he had to sleep alone, he didn't want to be driving.

Chapter Twelve

TGIF, Stonefield! A little birdie told the Gazette *we'll finally learn what's opening next to the Perkin' Up Café! The newspapers that have been covering the windows for so long will finally come down next week, and the town's most captivating mystery since the identity of the person smuggling chickens into the school will be solved!*

—Stonefield Gazette *Facebook Page*

The last thing Laura wanted to be doing tonight was sitting through book club—even one that included alcohol. But Books & Brews was special to the Sutton family, and to their circle of friends, so she'd gotten in Ellen's car even though she would rather have locked herself in her room and called Riley. Even if she couldn't see him, she could hear his voice.

Instead, she slowly sipped a beer and listened to the lively discussion. Usually she'd take part in it because talking books was one of her favorite things, and doing it in a bar instead of in a library was even more fun. But she couldn't stop thinking about Riley.

Ellen nudged her under the table, and when she looked over, her friend gave her a questioning look. "Are you paying attention?"

"Of course."

"No, you're not," Ellen whispered. "Why are you so distracted?"

She wanted to tell her. Ellen had been her best friend for most of her life, but she certainly couldn't tell her *here*. She also wasn't sure her friend would be happy for her.

She doesn't need to date anybody. She has me. We're going to be merry widows together and have all kinds of fun adventures.

It wasn't the first time Ellen had said something like that. In fact, she'd told Laura once that looking forward to them spending time together and doing all kinds of fun things they'd always wanted to do had helped her through the grief of losing her husband.

Even without the complications Riley's age and working for the tree service brought, she thought Ellen might not like her dating, period.

"Just thinking about work stuff," she whispered back. Not that the whispering helped. They were distracting the others, and when Callan cleared his throat, both women turned their attention back to him.

Then she saw Riley. He walked through the door and her breath caught in her chest. Her evening drastically improved when he entered, and the only thing that would make it perfect would be crossing the room and giving him a big kiss hello.

That would certainly spice up the conversation.

As people who'd just entered a neighborhood bar did, he scanned the room to see who was there, and his gaze locked with hers.

And he smiled.

She smiled back. It wasn't enough. She wanted to sit with him and hold his hand. Talk about his day. This sneaking-around stuff wasn't quite as exciting as fiction made it out to be. Especially when she hadn't figured out how to get him back in her bed yet.

Riley looked at the book club crowd around her and then winked at her before taking a seat at the bar. The text message appeared silently on her phone screen a few seconds later.

Tell them you feel like the book is an allegory for the social structure of a middle school cafeteria. Book clubs love allegories.

She laughed out loud and was rewarded with an elbow from Ellen and an arched eyebrow from Callan. The man was a sweetheart, but he had that stern librarian look locked down. Laura muttered an apology and slid her phone back into her bag.

She was tempted to get up and walk over to the bar. The book had been boring—not a single murder in it—and all she wanted to do was talk to Riley. But she'd come with Ellen, and she didn't want to let Callan down.

It could wait.

Finally, the conversation around her wound down. Callan and Molly introduced three choices for next month, and Laura was thrilled to see a thriller listed. It was definitely time to introduce some dead bodies to book club.

As the Books & Brews crowd started leaving, Laura racked her brain, trying to come up with any excuse to linger. She couldn't leave the bar without talking to Riley. It didn't even matter if they talked about the weather. She just needed to hear his voice. But even though she kept looking his way, she couldn't muster up the courage to go join him.

Then Ellen started gathering her things and Laura knew she was running out of time. She was going to have to walk right by Riley and keep walking, as if she hadn't spent the day desperately wanting to see him.

She turned to her friend. "I need to talk to Riley about that work stuff I was thinking about before I forget."

"Can't you send him an email?"

"Yeah, that works so well with these guys. And you don't have to wait."

Ellen frowned. "I drove, remember?"

"He'll bring me home." Eventually.

Eyes narrowing, Ellen leaned closer. "What are you doing, Laura Thompson?"

"Talking to one of the guys about work." But she wasn't a great liar, especially when talking to a woman who knew her so well.

"Nothing good will come of this, but you're an adult." Ellen shook her head. "I guess I'll talk to you soon, then."

Laura almost called her back. She could tell Ellen was a little put out at leaving alone. But she really wanted to talk to Riley. And if their relationship ever became not-a-secret, her friend would have to adjust, anyway.

After Ellen left, Laura gathered her things and joined Riley at the bar. She hung her bag from one of the hooks installed down the length of the bar and then slid onto the stool.

She leaned close to him, but not *too* close, because she didn't want to attract any more notice than her sitting with him already would. "I hope you're planning to buy me a beer, because I told my ride you'd drive me home."

He chuckled. "I walked from my place because I knew I'd have several tonight."

"Well. I didn't plan *that* very well, did I?" When Irish walked over to see if she wanted anything, she asked for a soda. "I had a beer because that's the point of Books & Brews, but I only had the one and it took me the entire meeting to drink it. But I guess that's irrelevant since I don't have a car."

"You can walk back with me," he said in a low voice. "The weather's going to be nice for the next week. You can take my truck home, and I'll ride my bike in tomorrow."

"I miss having a car. I'm going to have to make time for car shopping very soon, I guess."

"Like I said before, just tell me when. But in the meantime, I mean it—just take my truck."

Irish set her soda down on the bar, and Laura couldn't meet his eyes. She knew he was probably wondering why his mother-in-law's best friend was sitting with the tree service's new guy at his bar.

"Thank you," she told him.

"If you need a car, you know we can figure it out," Irish said, and she remembered the cowboy had very good hearing.

"She can use my truck," Riley assured him. "It's no big deal. We'll just walk back to my place and then she can drive it home."

Irish wasn't a very expressive man, but Laura could tell he was amused. Maybe Mallory had said something to him about that whole *too young for you* conversation.

"You okay?" Riley asked in a low voice when Irish had moved on.

She smiled, but it was a little forced. "Perfect."

* * *

Walking through the dark, quiet town with Laura would have been one of the most perfect moments of Riley's life if he could've held her hand. The distance between them felt like a chasm, but he knew if he threaded his fingers through hers, dark or not, somebody would see and Lane would probably hear about it before Laura even got home.

He hated it.

"I'm frustrated, too," she said quietly. "We'll figure it out."

He wasn't sure if she meant they'd figure out how to get each other naked again or how to break the news to the family, but he'd like for both to happen sooner rather than later.

"I know it's hard for you," he said. "I don't know many people here yet, so nobody really cares what I do."

The closer they got to the funeral home, the slower they walked. They were quiet for the most part, although she'd occasionally point to a business or a house and whisper stories about the owners. He was never going to remember them all, but he loved listening to her.

"You still need to finish reading that book to me, by the way," she said when they'd almost reached the final corner.

He chuckled. "You didn't bring it with you, did you?"

"No, but I still have it. And I haven't even peeked at the ending."

"Soon," he promised. "Maybe there will be a funeral and we can sneak you upstairs while they're distracted with the viewing."

She laughed, and he let the sound wash over him. "Please tell me you realize how wrong that is."

"It didn't come out as sexy as I'd hoped, no."

Then they were in the driveway, next to his truck, and it was time for the night to end. He didn't want it to, though. After fishing the keys out of his pocket, he pulled the truck's key and fob off the main ring and handed them to her.

"I want you to come up," he said. "But I know it's late. But if you come up here by the front of the truck, nobody can see us, so I can give you one quick kiss."

"A quick kiss. The later I am, the less likely all I did was walk here to borrow your truck. And Lane will worry if I'm too late, especially since the accident."

He chuckled. "I don't want that. Don't Piss Off a Man Who Owns a Commercial Wood Chipper is one of my mottoes in life."

"Lane would never run you through the chipper," she told him firmly. "Bone is a lot harder than wood, and he wouldn't want to nick the blades."

His laughter sounded loud in the quiet night, and he dropped his face to her shoulder to stifle it. Her body shook with her own barely restrained laughter, and he heard his truck key hit the ground as she wrapped her arms around him, running her hands up his back.

He lifted his head from her shoulder and cupped her face as he lowered his mouth to hers. Her lips were soft, parting for him, and he dipped his tongue between them. Her back was against the door of his truck, and he shifted so his knee was between her legs and the entire length of her body warmed his.

She moaned against his mouth and he very, very reluctantly broke off the kiss and backed up. "You should probably go before we forget why we're making sensible and responsible decisions."

"I think you're one kiss too late to prevent that," she said, her voice a little breathless. "But you're right. I should go."

He picked up his key and handed it to her a second time. Their fingers touched and lingered for a few seconds, but then she hit the button to unlock the door.

"You're sure I can take your truck?"

"Very sure. You can use it until you get a new car." He grinned. "Or until it drops below forty degrees. Whichever comes first."

"Thank you."

She climbed into the driver's seat, but before she could pull the door closed, he moved to block it. Stepping onto the running board, he leaned in and kissed her one more time because he couldn't help himself.

But he had to let her go, so he stepped back and

closed the door gently. She blew him a kiss as she put the truck in Reverse and backed onto the street. He watched her until she turned the corner and was out of sight. Then he walked toward the stairs, wishing he didn't have to care if anybody had seen them kissing.

Chapter Thirteen

We apologize to anybody who saw the photo briefly posted to our Page last night. A member of the staff (no, we won't tell you who) didn't realize they were signed into the work account when they uploaded it. They deleted it as soon as they realized. We're sorry for the mistake and wish to clarify that we do not endorse riding a motorcycle in a bikini.
—Stonefield Gazette *Facebook Page*

Laura heard a motorcycle engine in the distance, and she frowned when the sound cut off just as it neared the lower driveway. That was definitely Riley's bike—coasting now in case anybody was sleeping—and he was *very* early. She didn't think Lane and Evie had even come downstairs yet.

She hadn't seen either of them since last night, when her son had met her on the front porch, wanting to know why she was driving Riley's truck. She'd explained the situation to him, and he'd been justifiably confused. There were plenty of people she could have called for a ride. And she could have borrowed a car from somebody in the family—like his personal truck.

Telling him it was perfectly acceptable to borrow a truck from a man you were kind-of-dating wasn't an option, so she'd explained it away as the easiest thing to do at the time and told him not to worry about it. He hadn't liked that, but it wasn't really his business.

Her phone chimed with a text message from Riley. Are you up?

Of course. She hesitated for a few seconds, not liking the turn the morning was taking. Maybe he'd gotten up extra early so he could sneak a few minutes alone with her, but she didn't think so. Should I come say hi?

Yeah.

That was all she got, and by the time she'd put on her shoes and a sweater, her stomach was starting to ache. This was it, she thought. The end. The walk to the garage had never felt so long.

When she walked through the side door, she spotted Riley immediately. He was sitting on one of the metal folding chairs with his elbows on his knees and his head down. The door closed behind her and he looked up. The spark of happiness at seeing her couldn't disguise the weariness in his eyes.

He hadn't asked her down here to sneak a few kisses. He was going to tell her this was all too hard and they couldn't do it again. And she understood, but that didn't make it any easier.

"I can't keep doing this," he said in a low voice, confirming her fears.

"I know this is hard for you, Riley." She swallowed past the emotion trying to make a lump in her throat. She was *not* going to cry and make this harder for both of them. "I get it, and I don't blame you."

"I have to tell him."

Just the thought of Lane knowing what she and Riley had been up to made Laura's stomachache worse. If it was over, why tell him at all? "If you can't do this anymore, what do you gain by telling him?"

His brow furrowed, and then he shook his head. "When I said I can't do this, I meant I can't lie anymore. I worked with Case yesterday and it was hard. When I see Lane, it's even worse, and I can't keep doing it. I either have to tell him or I have to leave the company, but I can't see you behind his back and work for him at the same time."

Her breath left her in a rush. He wasn't breaking up with her. Not yet, anyway. Tears threatened again, and she blinked them away.

As hard as it was to hear, Laura didn't miss the fact that not seeing her anymore wasn't one of the options he listed for himself. Of course, if he left the company and kept seeing her, Lane would find out, anyway. And Riley leaving the tree service was the last thing she wanted to see happen.

"And after last night, you can't tell me we can go on this way," he continued. "I wanted to hold your hand while we walked. I don't want to have to hide behind my truck to kiss you."

"I know," she whispered. "But telling everybody will be hard."

"I have to do it."

"Would it be better if I told him?" she asked. She could do it—just casually drop that she was dating Riley and Lane should mind his own business.

"No." He chuckled, shrugging one shoulder. "I mean, yes. Obviously it would be easier for me if you told him, but that wouldn't sit right with me. I'll tell him."

"If it doesn't go well…give it a little time. He's very reactive and a little hotheaded, but once he calms down, he usually feels bad and tries to make it right."

"It is what it is." He looked at her a long time, and her breath caught in her chest when he unleashed that sexy grin she loved so much. "You're worth it."

The sentiment warmed her, but she didn't want his job and sense of security to be the price he paid for what they'd done.

"*We're* worth it," he added, and it was suddenly hard for her to swallow.

Was he hoping for more than she had to give? When he looked at her, did he see a future with wedding rings and baby blankets? She pulled the sweater tighter around herself to fight off the sudden chill.

"You should go, I guess. I'm not ready to have that conversation right now, so I don't want him to come looking for you."

"Okay." She sighed and tried to give him an encouraging smile, though she wasn't sure if she pulled it off. "Will you call me after?"

"I'll try."

There was nothing else to say, and Laura could tell by his body language he wasn't going to kiss her again until he'd talked to her son. There was nothing else to do but go back to the house and wait.

All day, all she could think about was Riley telling Lane about their relationship—running possible reactions over and over in her head until she wanted to scream. By the time Ellen stopped by to collect her empty casserole dishes, she was downright cranky and her friend could tell.

"What's going on with you?" she asked when they'd spent several minutes at the table with their tea and Laura hadn't said a word.

"Nothing."

The look Ellen gave her could have stripped paint off the wall. "Please. I know you better than that. Are you having headaches? Should you see your doctor?"

"No, my head is fine." Painwise, anyway. "There's just a lot going on. The accident. Dealing with insurance companies."

"I heard you're driving Riley's truck. And I see it's parked up here instead of in the pit."

Of course she'd already heard. The family grapevine didn't mess around. "He offered it, since he has his bike."

"You can borrow Evie's Jeep, though. Or you can take my car if you want. I can take Mallory's and she can drive that monster-sized pickup of Irish's."

"I'm fine with Riley's truck. Also, I slept with him." She hadn't meant to say it, but she couldn't hold it in. Not with Ellen.

"Oh."

"Yeah."

"I'm surprised you're so cranky, then. Did the content not live up to the promise of the packaging?"

Laura laughed. "Has Evie been giving you marketing lessons for the taproom again?"

"Oh, I think you know what I mean."

"I do, and…the content exceeded my expectations."

Ellen leaned back in her chair. "You do *not* look like a woman who's had her expectations exceeded."

"He's going to tell Lane."

"Good," Ellen said quickly, but then she frowned. "It *is* good, right?"

"I don't know." She shook her head. "No, I do know. It's good because Riley said if he didn't tell

Lane, he'd have to quit. He can't work with him with that secret between them. The problem is that I have no idea how Lane will take it."

"You're a grown woman. And as much as kids don't want to hear about it, moms get to have sex, too."

Laura laughed. "It's not so much about me having sex, as I think there's that guy code thing. Riley not only works for Lane, but if you asked Lane, he'd probably say they're kind of friends, too. And I'm pretty sure guys consider their mothers off-limits."

"Probably. When is he going to tell him?"

"I'm not sure, but probably today if he can get him alone. Irish has everything under control in the brewing room, so Lane was going out with the guys on today's job."

"I'm sure it will be fine. Lane's an adult, and he's also a business owner who isn't going to let a guy like Riley get away. Plus, he wants you to be happy."

Laura sipped her tea, hoping it would calm her stomach. She hoped Ellen was right, though she doubted it would be that easy. And all she could do was wait.

By the time Riley found the right place and time to tell Lane he was in a relationship with his mom— if a right place and time even existed—his stomach was in knots.

Having the conversation over a beer had sounded like a good idea, but the taproom wasn't private enough.

And he didn't want to knock on Lane's door and tell him in his home, because it was Laura's home, too. If Lane said something hurtful, he didn't want Laura to hear it.

That left the garage as the right place. The right time didn't come until the other guys had left. Case lingered, so Riley had to do the same. Clamping his chain saw to the table they used for the purpose, he took his time sharpening the blade. It gave him an excuse to still be there, and the steady rasp of the file calmed his nerves.

Until Case called for Boomer and headed for his truck. With every step man and dog took, Riley's anxiety ratcheted up another notch. He'd deliberately not rehearsed what he was going to say, and now he was wondering if that was a mistake. He'd wanted the conversation to happen naturally, and he'd hoped to take his cues from Lane, but now that it was time, he had no idea how to start.

"You look like a man with something on his mind," Lane said, solving *that* problem.

"I was hoping we could talk for a few minutes," Riley said, and then he exhaled slowly. "About Laura."

Lane frowned. "My mom? What about her?"

Riley would have preferred to have this discussion sitting down, rather than facing off across the utility table, but there was no turning back now. "She and I are... Well, we've gotten close."

Lane's eyebrows shot up before settling into a frown. "What the hell is that supposed to mean?"

"I guess you could say we're dating."

"Dating?" Lane shook his head. "No. My mom never dates, even when I tell her she should. She says she's happy with her life the way it is."

"She is happy. But she also enjoys spending time with me, and the feeling's mutual."

Lane shoved a hand through his hair, which made a mess of it because he was actively shaking his head when he did it. "I don't... No."

Lane's refusal to accept it was a disappointment, but his reaction was better than getting punched in the face, which had been a possibility Riley had considered. "I hope you can be okay with it. If not, I'll put in my notice."

"Or you could stop dating *my mom*."

"That's not going to happen."

When Lane glared at him, Riley didn't fidget or look away. Instead, he waited silently while the other man sorted through his emotions.

"When the hell did this start?"

"The attraction was there right away," he said, not surprised when Lane winced. "But after her accident, when you guys were away, we spent time together."

"When she had a damn concussion?" Lane took a step toward him, his hand curled into a fist, and Riley braced himself. "And here I was thinking you were just a nice guy, staying close in case she needed help."

"I was reading to her," he responded calmly, because he didn't want Lane thinking he'd taken advantage of Laura while she was in a weakened state. "She had a headache, but wanted to know what was going to happen next in her book."

Lane's hand relaxed, though the rest of his body remained rigid. "You were reading to her?"

"Yes." But he was going to put all his cards on the table today. "I did stay over the last night you were away, at her invitation."

For what felt like forever, but was probably only a minute, there was nothing but the sound of their breathing. Riley was silent, since he'd said what needed to be said, and at this point trying to explain more would probably only make it worse. And he wasn't sorry he was with Laura, so he couldn't even apologize for it.

"Dammit, Riley." Lane turned away, walking to the fridge in the back of the garage. He pulled out a crowler of the Sutton's Place house ale and poured it into two plastic cups.

Riley took the one offered to him with a nod of thanks. He wasn't going to speak again until Lane did because it was the only way to guarantee he didn't say the wrong thing.

"I don't want you to quit," Lane said finally, and relief eased Riley's tension enough so he could take a sip of the beer without fear of choking. "You're a good fit here, and I don't think we'd find somebody good enough to replace you."

"I appreciate that, and I don't want to quit, either."

"But you're going to keep dating my mom." Lane sighed when he nodded. "You're my age."

"Not really."

"Okay, but you're not *her* age."

"No, but I'm close enough so it doesn't matter."

Lane took another long swallow of beer. "Is it serious?"

That was a good question, and one he couldn't answer. "We enjoy being together. That's all I can really say."

"Why tell me, then? There's that saying, ignorance is bliss, and I think that definitely applied here."

"It felt wrong to me. I wasn't lying, but it felt like a secret I was keeping from you. I respect you as a boss, I like you on a personal level, and I know how close you and Laura are. I didn't feel like I could look you in the eye." Riley sighed. "And she shouldn't have to sneak around like that. If she's doing something that makes her happy, she shouldn't have to hide it from her family and her friends."

Lane's jaw tightened as he inhaled slowly. "Case told me he thought it was weird you were hanging around the garage like that, but I laughed it off. I guess I should have listened to him."

"I *was* there to be close because I hated her being alone after the accident. I was actually getting ready to leave when she said she was in the middle of a good book and reading gave her a headache."

Something in Lane's expression softened for a moment, which was what Riley had hoped for. He didn't want to be seen as a horny dog sniffing around Lane's mother. He was a good guy, and his interest in Laura went a lot deeper than that.

He wasn't sure *how* deep yet, but he wanted the chance to find out.

"Case said you seemed off on Tuesday. That you were in the office, and when you came out, you seemed jumpy, and that you were quiet all day."

"Because I didn't get there early. I spent the night." Lane's jaw clenched, but he didn't say anything. "And it felt wrong to lie to him, and I knew it would feel even more wrong to lie to you, so here we are."

"Here we are," Lane echoed, and then he sighed. "I know the right thing to say here. My mother's... *personal* life is none of my business."

"But it's weird," Riley finished for him.

"Of course it's weird, dude. She's my *mom*."

"I know. Trust me, it's weird for me, too. But I can't help it. She's—"

"No." Lane held up his hand, shaking his head. "Nope. I like you and I love my mother and I respect you both, so I'm going to keep myself out of it, but that also means *you* keep me out of it."

"Fair enough. I was just going to say that she's amazing."

Lane nodded. "Well, she is that, for sure."

The conversation had run its course for now, so Riley tossed his empty cup into the garbage can. "I guess I'll see you in the morning, then."

After a few seconds, Lane set his cup down and

stood. "I'm not going to lie to you. This will be weird for a while. But I respect you for telling me, and the bottom line for me will always be my mother's happiness. If you're making her happy, then that's what's important, I guess."

"If I stop making her happy, she'll let me know."

"It's going to take me some time to wrap my head around this." Lane frowned. "Who else knows?"

Riley shrugged one shoulder. "I think Ellen knows. I don't know if Evie or her sisters do."

Lane shook his head. "Damn Sutton women. They're way too good at keeping secrets. I never know how much they know about anything."

Riley felt as though a massive weight had dropped from his shoulders at the hint of amusement in his boss's voice. Of course, now there was a little voice in his head pointing out this could all go sideways again if things between him and Laura *didn't* work out, but that was a worry for another day.

After parting ways with his boss and taking the long way home, he parked his bike in the funeral home driveway and tried to call Laura, but it went to voice mail. Assuming she might be talking to Lane or eating dinner, he sent her a text message. That was hard, but the good news is he took it better than I expected.

A few minutes later, her response came through. What's the bad news?

I have to work tomorrow.

She sent the laughing emoji, and he waited, but there were no dots to indicate she was typing. When he couldn't take it anymore, he sent another text.

I want to take you on a real date.

Okay, how about being my official plus-one to Evie's birthday barbecue? Everybody will know by then, anyway.

Riley sighed. He'd meant a nice dinner and maybe a walk around town—Stonefield didn't have a super exciting nightlife—rather than being surrounded by her family and friends all at once.

But he couldn't tell Laura no. And she wasn't wrong about everybody knowing about their relationship by then. If the barbecue would be the first time she'd have to face them all, he was going to be there to hold her hand.

Plus, he'd have leverage when it came time to invite her to his mother's birthday gathering.

It's a date.

Chapter Fourteen

Stonefield officially has a new business! John Fletcher has taken the newspaper out of the windows to reveal Fletcher Digital Restoration and Design! According to John, his primary business is digital design, with most of his work for clients done remotely. But moving to Stonefield to be closer to his brother (most of you know Bruce!) and opening an office is allowing him to pursue his passion of restoring old photos that are fading or have been damaged. If you have old pictures that are creased, peeling, water damaged or are just getting worn with time, stop by and John will give you an estimate on preserving your precious memories!
—Stonefield Gazette *Facebook Page*

When Laura heard her phone chime four times in under two minutes while she was in the shower, she knew something was up. Not something horrible, or the phone would actually ring, but somebody definitely wanted to talk to her.

Not Riley. He'd send one message and then wait for a response because he knew she might be with her family or working, or she might have Becca. He knew she'd respond as soon as she could.

And since it wasn't Riley, and it wasn't an emergency, she took her time rinsing off. Then she wrapped her hair in a towel and, after drying off, slid on her thick robe. Only then did she pick up her phone and read the text messages. They were all from Ellen, sent one right after the other. She didn't love texting, so she was probably holding a sleeping Leeza.

Evie told Mallory that Lane finally knows about you and Riley!

How did he really take it? Evie said he didn't want to talk about it last night, but he didn't seem mad.

Does this mean you two are officially a couple now?

It's not a secret anymore, right?

Sighing, Laura went into her bedroom and sat on the edge of the bed to answer her friend's questions.

Lane took it pretty well. He said it's weird, but he didn't fire Riley, so that's good. I guess we're a couple? And more than two people know, so of course it's not a secret. I'd rather everybody didn't gossip about us, though.

Good luck with that. And I'm happy for you.

Thanks! That means a lot to me. And it did, even if she wasn't totally sure her friend truly meant those words.

When she got back a heart emoji, Laura knew the conversation was over, so she hurried to get dressed. She was hoping to run into Lane before he went down to the garage, just to gauge his mood. She hadn't seen him since Riley talked to him, and it was bugging her. And she wanted to make sure he hadn't stewed about it all night and changed his mind about being cool with Riley.

She was running late, though, so she didn't bother with her hair, other than running a wide-tooth comb through it. It would be a mess later, but it was going to end up in a scrunchie, anyway.

The creaking of floorboards and the low murmur of indecipherable voices over her head told Laura that Lane and Evie had gone upstairs to get dressed after breakfast, so she went to the kitchen to make herself a coffee. She'd just taken her first sip when her cell phone told her she had a text message from Riley.

I can't find the paper I wrote the gate access code for today's job on. Did you see it in the stuff I turned in last night?

She thought about it for a few seconds and had another sip of coffee. I think there was a number written at the bottom of one. They're on my desk, so you can come up and look through them.

Be right there.

Shameless, she thought. Rather than walking into the office, finding the number and sending it to him, she was making him walk up to the house just so she'd get to see him.

A few minutes later, there was a quick knock on the door, and then she heard it open and close. Footsteps heading toward her office.

"I'm in the kitchen," she called to him, reveling in the thrill of being free to do that. They were an item now, which meant he could see her in other parts of the house than just the office.

"Just a sec," he called back, and she traced the sound of his footsteps to the office. He wasn't in there long before she heard him leaving, presumably with the gate code.

When he walked into the kitchen, her mood lifted just from seeing his face. Not that it had been bad to start with, but seeing that smile made the day instantly better.

"Did you find it?"

He nodded. "Yeah. I know better than to use paper-work as a scratch pad, but at least I don't have to call the customer and tell him I lost his gate code."

When he kept coming, crossing the kitchen, she set her coffee on the counter so she could wrap her arms around his neck. He grinned down at her as he ran his fingers through the wet length of her hair. Then he lifted the strands to his face and inhaled deeply.

"I love the smell of your shampoo," he confessed.

"Not weird at all to find an employee in my kitchen, smelling my mom's hair," she heard Lane say, and she felt bad when she saw the anxiety flash through Riley's eyes as he dropped her hair and took a step back. He didn't know Lane well enough to hear the wry humor in his tone.

"He's got three more minutes before the work-day technically starts," Laura told her son, and she took Riley's hand to keep him from moving too far away from her. "When he's here off the clock, he's with me."

"I don't care that he's with you. I care about him smelling your hair in front of me," Lane grumbled.

Evie was right behind him, holding Becca, and she laughed. "Like your mom didn't have to count ceiling tiles the other night when I bent over to pick up that napkin I dropped and you got grabby."

They all laughed, even Riley, and Lane gave his wife a sheepish grin. "Okay, you've got me there."

Laura caught Riley's eye, and he winked at her. Relieved he was okay with the teasing, she squeezed his hand and gave him a smile.

"Time to go to work," Lane said. He kissed Becca's cheek and then Evie's mouth. "You ready, Riley?"

"Sure thing," he said, and he started to pull away.

Laura still had his hand, and she used it to pull him back to her. Then she cupped his face and kissed him until Lane made a low growling sound and then an *oof* sound, as if his wife had elbowed him or stomped on his foot.

Then she ran her thumb across his bottom lip. "Have a good day at work."

The tips of his ears were pink as he followed Lane out of the kitchen, but he turned back to give her a look that promised she was going to pay for that later in all the best possible ways. She couldn't wait.

"I almost wish I was going with them," Evie said once they were gone. "That was funny."

"I want Riley to stick around, so Lane's just going to have to get used to it."

"Good for you, Laura." She bounced Becca lightly, since she was starting to fuss. "You deserve to have some fun. And to be happy, and anybody can see that he makes you *very* happy."

Yes, he did, she thought as she moved to the window so she could watch him walk away.

Riley walked alongside Lane as they made their way down to the garage. Case's truck was pulling in and, as far as Riley could tell, all the other guys had arrived. Bruce's crew was already in their trucks and would be pulling out once Case's truck was out of the way.

"You know, you can take your truck back," Lane said. "We have enough vehicles in the family so Mom doesn't need it."

"So I've been told, but I don't mind her using it." Quite the opposite, actually. He liked imagining her driving his truck while he was at work. "She can keep it until she gets a new car for herself sorted."

Lane snorted. "I hope you've got snow tires for that Harley. She loved her car, and she's dragging her feet on finding another one."

"I told her I have some connections with one of those big lots that have a little of everything, and we'd take her favorite tumbler with us, and she can sit in every one of them until she finds the perfect cup holder."

Lane stopped walking abruptly, so Riley also stopped. He turned to find his boss looking at him intently, but he couldn't decipher his expression. Then he smiled and shook his head. "That's my mom. She's convinced no other car will have just the right cup holder and center console, and in the emergency room, she was worried about the library books in the back seat."

Riley chuckled because that didn't surprise him in the least. They started walking again, and Boomer ran to greet them. He went to Lane first, of course, but then he went to Riley for his daily greeting.

The dog's human wasn't quite as thrilled to see him, though. Case's jaw was set, and he greeted Riley with a short nod before turning his back to fill the jug in his back seat with ice and water from the garage.

Riley followed him, thankful the others were out in the yard. "Hey, Case. I'm sorry I didn't say anything to you even though we worked together. I felt like I had to tell Lane myself, and that wasn't a secret I could have asked you to keep from him until I had the chance."

Case turned and stared at him for a few seconds before chuckling. "You've got a knack for saying the right thing, don't you? I think that's pretty much the only thing you could have said that would make me not pissed about it. I couldn't have kept that from Lane, and I respect that you saw that and that you wanted to tell him yourself."

"Are we good?"

"Yeah, we're good." Then he gave Riley a pointed look. "As long as Aunt Laura's good, we're good."

And there it was again—that knot of pressure in his gut. He'd expended so much mental energy worrying about Lane and Case being okay with him dating Laura that he hadn't thought about how much worse it could be if they broke up down the road. He couldn't imagine things ever getting unpleasant between him and Laura, even if it didn't work out, but that didn't mean the men in her life would take it well.

They all went their separate ways for the day, with Case and Riley running two different jobs and Lane spending the day at the brewery. Or that was the plan, anyway. Midafternoon, Riley got a call from Lane. A car accident had taken out a tree *and* an electrical pole. D&T Tree Service could work with live wires, so they'd gotten the call to assist the fire department and the power company, and it was a priority job. They wanted him there.

After giving his crew instructions on how to finish their task, Riley was ready when Lane pulled up in front of the customer's driveway. He climbed into the passenger seat and held on as his boss made an illegal U-turn.

It was almost dark by the time the accident scene was cleared. After finishing their job, Neil and Shane had shown up with the chipper, and even they'd gotten done and gone home before the power company released them.

Riley, Lane and Case stood on the side of the road, chugging water. Case had dropped Boomer off at home with his wife on the way, so Riley didn't even have the dog to interact with. There was still some tension in the air, which he'd expected. It would take some time for them to get used to his relationship, and he'd be patient. But it was a lot easier feeling on the outside when there was a dog looking for a belly rub.

"So Gwen's pregnant," Case said, and when Lane didn't react other than grinning at his cousin, Riley realized he'd been talking to him.

"Congratulations," he said, slapping Case on the shoulder. "Ellen's going to have her hands full, but cousins are cool, and having Becca, Leeza and your baby be relatively close in age will be awesome as they grow up."

Case's grin couldn't have been wider. "We're pretty excited about it. Lane and I are going to the taproom tomorrow night to celebrate with Irish, if you want to come along."

He did, but he looked to Lane to see how *he* felt about it. Forcing himself into a family situation wasn't going to make the awkwardness better.

"I wouldn't have invited you without checking with him first," Case said.

"It's cool," Lane said. "We're just going to have a couple of beers and talk about babies."

"I have five nieces and nephews, so I should be able to contribute something to the conversation."

When both men gave him speculative looks, he knew what they were thinking. He didn't have kids of his own. He was dating a woman whose son was definitely grown. And they wanted to know what that meant for him.

He didn't know, so he didn't say anything.

"You can buy a round," Lane said, clapping him on the back while Case laughed.

"And nachos," Case added, and they were all laughing when they split off to the two trucks.

Riley slid into the passenger seat of Lane's truck and pulled his phone out. He wanted to tell Laura about the invite to join the guys at the taproom. But he couldn't really talk to her on the phone while Lane was driving, and he tended to get motion sickness pretty quickly if he used his phone in a moving vehicle.

He'd wait until they got back to the garage. Maybe they could sit on the porch or on the swing in the backyard and he could tell her. It would ease her mind, knowing Lane and Case were still including him socially.

It was going to be okay.

Chapter Fifteen

Dearborn's Market was closed for several hours today after a possible hazmat call was made to the fire department. After evacuating the store and conducting a thorough investigation, it was determined that, unbeknownst to the market staff, a very large jar of sauerkraut had fallen off the back of a shelf and broke. The incident coincided with a temporary failure of the air-conditioning system, resulting in an unknown (but very pungent) odor. After cleaning up the sauerkraut, an attempt was made to cover the smell with an air freshener that promised to smell like a Hawaiian breeze. The management offered this statement: "Look, the store doesn't smell good right now. It's pretty bad. But we

*have perishables to move, so we'll be offering
10 percent off all purchases (except tobacco
and alcohol) for the next two days."*
          —Stonefield Gazette *Facebook Page*

Laura stepped through the door of the Perkin' Up
Café and paused for a few seconds to inhale the
fresh, rich scent of coffee. It was Friday morning, it
had been a long week and she was still waiting on a
call back from her insurance company, so she was
treating herself.

Before Chelsea had opened the first—and only—
coffee shop in Stonefield several years ago, Laura
had been content with a mug of plain old coffee with
two sugars and a splash of half-and-half.

Then Chelsea had introduced them all to the won-
ders of lattes and espresso and foam, and Laura's caffeine intake would never be the same again.

"I think an iced cappuccino today," she said when
it was her turn.

"Maybe with an extra shot of espresso?"

Laura laughed. "Do I look that tired?"

"You look gorgeous, but you might need an extra
boost if you're going to keep up with that younger
man of yours."

Laura's face froze as her breath caught in her chest.
Chelsea already knew? That meant everybody did,
and gossip was a lot less fun when you were the topic
of conversation.

Chelsea's cheeks flamed and she put her hand

over Laura's. "I'm sorry. I was teasing. I didn't think it would bother you, and I'm seriously very sorry."

"No, it's fine." She managed a slightly ragged chuckle. "It's not a huge secret or anything. I just didn't realize everybody knew."

"Are you new in this town?" She laughed as she walked away to make Laura's drink.

She stood and waited. Usually, she'd look around and wave hello to the people she knew—which was usually everybody. But suddenly she was afraid if she turned, she'd find everybody staring at her. Maybe whispering about her and Riley.

She told herself not to care, but that was a lot easier said than done.

"I'm not sure *everybody* knows," Chelsea said while they waited for her card reader to process the transaction. "But since Riley moved into the apartment, he basically lives between Molly and her mother. You've been seen there. Plus, one of the Suttons told Molly."

"I love Molly, and she'll take a secret to her grave if you ask her to, but if you don't, forget it."

"So, sure, there are people talking, but it's a circle of people who care about you."

Laura couldn't hold back the question. "What does that circle of people think about it?"

"You shouldn't care, but everybody loves seeing you have a little fun."

She forced herself to smile as a new customer entered. "Thanks, Chelsea."

The smile faded as soon as the barista went to make a latte. *Have a little fun.*

So the people who knew her the best assumed she was simply indulging in a fling with a younger man. Even her friends didn't stop to consider that it might be more than a little fun.

When Chelsea came back from making the other customer's drink, she didn't look amused anymore, but she didn't say anything until the transaction was done and they were alone at the counter again. She glared at something over Laura's shoulder. "He's such a jerk."

Laura frowned, looking around the coffee shop to see if one of the customers was doing something wrong. "Who's a jerk?"

Chelsea made the kind of face often used for discovering dog poo on the bottom of one's shoes. "John Fletcher."

"That's Bruce's brother, right? The one that just moved to town?"

"And opened a business right next door to mine? Yes. That's the one, and he's a jerk. You should see the look he just gave me when he walked by my window. He's grumpy and judgmental, and he barks at me."

"Literally?"

Chelsea snorted. "No, not literally. I'd probably like him more if he was literally barking, but he just has that kind of voice that's harsh and bossy. And he doesn't like coffee."

"Oh, well, then." Laura shook her head. "He's gotta go."

"I wish."

"Maybe he doesn't mean to bark, though. It might be in the DNA. I mean, you know Bruce. He's not great at communication, either."

"But Bruce is nice. Quiet and he doesn't like to talk, but he's nice. His brother *does* like to talk, but nothing good comes out of his mouth."

Laura sipped her drink, not sure what to say to that. Chelsea got along with everybody. She'd become especially good friends with Molly, but she was liked by everybody in Stonefield, and it was good for her business to have a friendly smile for everybody. John Fletcher must *really* have gotten on her nerves.

"I don't want to talk about him anymore," Chelsea said, waving the subject of her grumpy business neighbor away with a flick of her hand. "I like talking about you and Riley McLaughlin more. Amanda says he's a super nice guy."

"He's very nice, yes."

"Okay, but not *too* nice, right?" Chelsea leaned across the counter as the bell over the door announced another customer was coming. "If you know what I mean."

"I know what you mean, and I'm not telling."

"Come on, Laura. I'm lonely. Give me something."

"If you like not-super-nice guys, there's a new one next door," she teased.

Chelsea snorted. "I'd duct-tape my knees together before I let John Fletcher get in there."

Whoever had walked through the door cleared his throat, and Laura knew before she turned who it was.

John Fletcher was a taller, more attractive version of his brother. The scowl was the same, though. "Duct tape will definitely not be necessary."

Laura expected Chelsea to blush or stammer some kind of explanation, but she only arched an eyebrow. "What can I do for you?"

"You can plug whatever machine you just used into a different outlet, because every time you use it, it dims my lights for a few seconds."

"No."

He looked taken aback. "No?"

"If you have an electrical issue, take it up with the landlord. The machines are set up for my workflow, and the previous tenants never complained. Maybe you're just too sensitive."

"To dimming lights while doing graphic design on a computer screen? Yes, I'm sensitive to that."

She shrugged. "Like I said, that's the landlord's problem."

"I'll take it up with him, then."

He turned around and left without another word, and Chelsea sagged against the counter. "See? He's a jerk. I swear, if I have to shut down so they can rewire this place, I'm going to be so mad."

"I doubt it will come to that. But I have to run. I promised Ellen I'd meet her at the library, and I got distracted by the whole duct-tape thing, and now I'm running late."

"I meant that," Chelsea said, hands on her hips.

Laura laughed. "I think he got the message."

Because she'd parked Riley's truck across two spots—risking a ticket and the wrath of the community, but it was a *lot* bigger than her car had been—Laura drove it to the library parking lot rather than walking from the café. Ellen was already there, waiting for her by the front steps, but Laura took her time turning off the engine and gathering her things.

Driving Riley's truck felt like such a *couple* thing, and she liked seeing her bag on the seat next to his sweatshirt. Her coffee sat in the center console next to a reusable water bottle he probably should take in and wash.

It all made her feel closer to him, and she closed her eyes for a moment, breathing in the scent of him that surrounded her, before reluctantly opening the door and climbing out.

Riley almost canceled going to the taproom with the guys. As important as it was to get back on equal footing with his bosses, what he really wanted to do was curl up in bed with Laura. He wanted to finish reading her that book—he still didn't know who the killer was—and then make love to her. Or sex first and then reading. The order didn't matter, as long as he was with her.

But he'd managed to catch a few minutes with her

at the end of the day. She'd spent the morning with Ellen, and then a good part of the afternoon arguing with her insurance company. The annoyance with them eased out of her muscles when he kissed her like a man who'd been dreaming of doing just that all day would—because he had.

But in order for Irish to be able to relax with the guys, Evie was working the bar for him. That meant Laura would be watching Becca for the evening. Reading was still on the table, but there would be no sneaking off to her room. He didn't mind and had offered to keep her company, but it had been more important to her that he go out with Lane and Case, and hopefully have a good time.

So far, it was going okay. Callan Avery, the librarian, had joined them since Molly was serving tonight. Molly had been best friends with Mallory growing up, and she was practically a fourth Sutton sister, from what he'd heard. It was a tight group, but he felt welcome, and by the end of the first beer, he was relaxed and enjoying himself.

"Hey, Callan, how's the wedding planning going?" Case asked.

When the librarian groaned and dropped his head as he shook it, they all laughed. "Planning anything with Molly is an adventure, but wedding planning? Last night she asked me if I thought we could get our entire guest list—which changes daily, of course— to go along with making our wedding a musical."

"We've done a few karaoke nights here in the tap-room," Irish said. "You don't want that."

"With choreographed dance routines."

"You *definitely* don't want that," Lane said. "Have you considered just running off to Vegas?"

"Or just running off?" Case added, and they all laughed. It was a safe joke because they knew running away from Molly was the last thing Callan would ever do, no matter how chaotic the wedding planning got.

"I'm begging you not to mention Las Vegas to Molly. If she gets it in her head our ceremony could be a musical starring Elvis, she'll want that. And of course, she'll want us to bring all of her friends and family with us so they can be in the number. My salary is public record, guys. No Vegas."

"I thought she wanted to get married in the gazebo in the town square," Irish said.

"That was last month. And she might want to again next month. She's following about two hundred wedding Instagram accounts too many. And Amanda, who has a slight obsession with painting things, has been complaining about the condition of the gazebo all summer. I'm surprised she hasn't snuck over in the middle of the night and painted it herself."

They stopped talking while Evie brought them another round, and Riley appreciated the warm smile she gave him.

"Have you guys talked about names yet?" Lane asked Case, bringing the conversation back to the reason they were celebrating.

"No. She says it's too soon. She didn't want to tell anybody yet, actually, but there's no way to hide the morning sickness. Or the afternoon sickness, or the middle-of-the-night sickness. Let's just say this kid needs a great name, because there's a good chance she's not doing this again."

Lane leaned across the table. "I'll give you a hundred dollars if you suggest the name Aspen."

Case groaned, and then caught Riley's curious look. "My wife's breakout novel was titled *A Quaking of Aspens*, and some people in Stonefield—like most of them—thought it was about them. She got so sick of hearing about it, she moved to Vermont. After David died and they had to get the brewery up and running, she came back to help. She fell in love with Boomer, and we're a package deal, so she stayed. But, anyway, Lane's a smart-ass."

Irish laughed. "I'll throw in a hundred."

"What the hell?" Riley said. "I'm in."

They all looked at Callan, who shook his head. "Again, librarian's salary. Wedding plans. Molly. I can't afford to be a pain in Case's ass."

Riley's phone chimed, and he pulled it out of his pocket to see a text message from Laura.

How's it going?

He smiled and set down his beer so he had both thumbs free to respond. We're having a good time. They're funny guys. I still wish I was with you, though.

There was a cereal situation. And a diaper situation. Also a ketchup situation but that was my own doing. If I can get her settled down, I'm going to try to jump in the shower.

He chuckled at the image of her the text brought to his mind. She sounded like a mess. You're not making me not want to be with you, though.

Soon. Preferably when I don't feel like the least sexy woman on the planet.

Never.

"Are you texting?" Case demanded, and Riley gave a sheepish smile as he slid the phone back into his pocket.

"Sorry. It was Laura. She's getting in the shower because—"

"Nope."

Riley stopped talking, scowling at Lane's hand, which he'd held up in a *stop* gesture. "Nope? Nope what?"

"You don't get to talk about your girlfriend texting you she's getting in the shower, because she's, you know, *my mom*."

"She's getting in the shower because there was a diaper incident and also something involving cereal and ketchup, so it wasn't exactly a booty call."

Case shook his head. "Never say 'booty call' again."

"Why did Becca have ketchup?" Lane asked, and they all looked at Riley because it was a valid question.

"The ketchup was self-inflicted, I guess. The rest was all Becca."

"She messaged you to tell you how gross she is right now?" Callan asked.

Irish snorted. "I guess it *is* a real relationship."

They all laughed, though Riley had to force his a little. Had there been doubt it was real? Maybe it was his age, but there seemed to be an assumption he and Laura were just having a quick fling. He wasn't sure exactly what they were doing yet, but if he had his way, it wasn't going to be quick.

When Evie brought the double order of nachos they'd asked for, she looked directly at Riley. "Are you coming to my birthday barbecue on Monday?"

"I... Laura did mention a barbecue." He should tell her he'd already agreed to be Laura's plus-one, but he felt a little on the spot, and he didn't want Laura to get any blowback if they felt she shouldn't have invited him to a family thing yet.

"My birthday's tomorrow, but between the thrift store and the brewery, it's pretty impossible to do things on a Saturday. Both of those are closed on Mondays, and Laura promised to have Case and Lane back by midafternoon, which means you'll be free. I hope you'll come."

Riley resisted looking at the other guys to gauge

how they felt about it. They were supposedly good. Laura wanted him to go with her. And Evie had invited him. He didn't need their permission to accept.

"I'll be there," he said, and she smiled before walking away.

He blew out a breath and leaned back in his chair before taking a long swallow of beer. Things might be a little touchy with the guys, but it sure seemed like the women in Laura's life were willing to accept him. Even though he'd already planned to attend the barbecue, it meant a lot to him that Evie went out of her way to invite him personally—especially in front of the guys. Now there was no doubt he was welcome there.

And then there would be his mom's birthday to look forward to. He wanted to bring Laura home to his family. She had a life full of people she loved, and he wanted her to meet the people *he* loved. And he wanted them to meet her.

"Three hundred dollars, huh?" Case mused, and Riley realized he was still thinking about poking the pregnant bear.

"Don't do it," Lane said, shaking his head. "It's not worth it."

"Three hundred dollars, though."

"If you do it," Irish said, "you have to video it to get the money."

"Proof you did it," Riley said.

"And evidence in her murder trial," Lane added. When Callan choked on his beer, Riley thumped him on the back while they all laughed. Then he got Evie's attention and signaled for another round. It was going to be a long night, but a good one.

Chapter Sixteen

Good news, Stonefield! That yellow tape around the gazebo isn't crime scene tape. It's closed for repainting! After several meetings and an investigation, it was determined the job wasn't left off of the budget. It was accidentally re-allocated to the town administrator's expense account. The mistake has been rectified and painting will commence on Monday!
— Stonefield Gazette *Facebook Page*

Everybody knowing Riley and Laura were seeing each other was one thing. But being in the middle of a big family celebration as Laura's date was a whole new level of scrutiny he'd thought he was prepared for.

He wasn't.

Evie's birthday barbecue was basically a gathering of all the people Laura cared about in the world, and they were all looking at him. Not all at the same time, thankfully. He probably would have apologized to Laura and then run away. But there were a lot of sideways glances and whispered comments.

They were all friendly, though, so he tried to ignore the chatter and focus on having a good time. And he knew enough of the guys, so he wasn't standing around with nobody to talk to. Lane and Case were there, of course. And Irish, who lived there. Callan and Molly.

Laura had gotten pulled into setting out the food. There was a big gazebo in the Suttons' backyard, with a massive picnic table where they seemed to be putting out dish after dish, as well as buns and condiments for the burgers and dogs on the grill. Lane and Case were handling that, so he walked over to Irish, who was watching his stepsons setting up the cornhole boards.

"You play?" Irish asked.

"Not well," he confessed. "And those boys look like they take it very seriously, so I don't think I stand a chance of a win today."

"They're merciless, too. They get that from their mother." He chuckled and tipped his hat back slightly as he looked sideways at Riley. "You enjoying yourself?"

"Yeah. Good people. Helluva lot of food. It's my kind of party."

"You've given people something to talk about, which is fun."

Riley laughed and shook his head. "That I did. I knew there would be a lot of talk, but I kind of thought they'd have it out of their systems by now."

"You could say they got the talk about Laura having a fling with a younger guy who works for the tree service out of their systems." Irish looked sideways at him. "But the talk about Laura being in a serious enough relationship to have the man come to a family birthday party is pretty fresh."

Riley frowned, letting the other man's words sink in and remembering what had been said at the taproom Friday night. They had all thought Laura was just having a fling with him. Did *she* think that?

"Burgers are done," Lane called, and everybody started migrating toward the gazebo.

Riley and Irish weren't even halfway across the yard when their phones chimed at the same time with text messages from Case.

Meet me behind the carriage house real quick while everybody's distracted.

"This should be interesting," Irish said, changing course.

It was a few minutes before Case and Lane appeared, with Callan right behind them. Riley was pretty sure that whatever they were about to do, they were going to get caught doing it, because the party guests were going to notice that all five of them went missing at the same time.

"This has got to be quick," Case said, pulling his phone out of his back pocket.

He tapped the screen a couple of times, and then held it up sideways to make the video full-screen. They were watching the Danforth kitchen, and they could see Gwen at the stove.

"You didn't," Lane said, his voice mirroring the disbelief they were probably all feeling.

"I had a pocket T-shirt on, so I put a tissue in the bottom of the pocket to keep the phone lens above the fabric."

Riley didn't know the oldest Sutton sister very well, but he'd gotten the impression it wasn't really a good idea to push her buttons. And since Case had gathered them in secret to watch this video, he suspected he was about to see her husband pushing the hell out of her buttons.

"I've been thinking about names," they heard Case say, and Gwen—who was in the process of plating spaghetti—sighed. "You know what would be cool? If it's a girl, we should name her Aspen."

On the screen, Gwen froze for so long, Riley wondered if the video playback had glitched. Then she turned a glare on Case—and the camera—that they all felt. Riley wondered if Case had turned the volume down on his phone, because there was a strong possibility they were about to hear a lot of yelling, but she just kept glaring and then shaking her head.

They all gasped when she picked up the two plates full of spaghetti with meatballs in red sauce, walked to the garbage can, used the foot pedal to open it and then dropped both plates in.

Then she whirled and stormed out, with the camera bouncing as Case went after her, and they could hear him pleading with her.

"Honey, it was a joke. I didn't mean it." She didn't even slow down. "Honey, come on. It was Lane's idea."

"Hey!" Lane backhanded him in the gut, and Case made an *oof* sound and dropped his phone.

"Oh, come on," Irish said. "She already knew that, as soon as the words came out of his mouth."

Lane shrugged. "Probably."

"That was worth a hundred dollars," Riley said as Case picked up his phone and the video went to black.

"You're fired."

Lane's phone chimed, and he looked at the text message. "They want to know where we are."

"And I'm hungry," Irish said.

"If anybody asks what we were doing," Case said, "Lane wanted to show us a nasty rash in a private place."

This time he was ready and dodged Lane's hand, but they were all laughing as they stepped out from behind the carriage house and headed toward the gazebo.

"Wait," Callan said. "Are we actually saying that?"

* * *

Laura felt torn in two directions. She wanted to be with Riley, who had been watching Mallory's boys play cornhole before heading over to check out the gazebo alone, but Ellen was sitting with her daughters and there was an empty chair beside her. Everybody knew that was Laura's chair. It was where they always sat after everybody had eaten, so they could rest for a while before the task of cleaning up commenced.

Guilt knotted her stomach, but it wasn't as if Ellen was alone. She was sitting with her daughters and holding her granddaughter, who was a tiny bundle of blanket. Riley was Laura's guest, so it would be rude not to make sure he was having a good time.

"Hey, you," she said as she reached his side.

"Hey. This is quite a gazebo."

"Yeah. Before David and Ellen bought this house, it was an inn, and they used to host weddings and stuff. The gazebo made for a nice photo setting, and now it's for family barbecues and long conversations."

"Long conversations, huh?"

"Sometimes it's the only private place to *have* a conversation around here."

He walked up the steps, then turned back to see if she was following. She was. "Are we going to have a long conversation that requires privacy?"

He chuckled. "Privacy? Not so much. But shade is nice."

They sat next to each other on the built-in bench,

facing the yard instead of the river so they'd know if anybody was joining them. Her hand found his, and their fingers laced together as if it was the most natural thing in the world.

"How do you feel about motorcycles?" he asked, nudging her shoulder with his.

"I don't know, really, other than thinking you look hot as hell on yours." She nudged him back. "My husband had one when we got married. He ended up selling it to put the money toward equipment to open the tree service."

"Did you ride with him?"

She shrugged. "Twice, I think, before I got pregnant with Lane. My parents didn't like him, and they *really* didn't like his motorcycle, so I had to sneak out and walk to the end of the road. Then he'd let the bike coast down the hill until we were far enough away from the house to start it."

He chuckled. "What about dropping you off? You can't kill the engine and coast a bike uphill."

"It was a very long walk home."

"What about after you got married?"

She pressed her lips together for a few seconds, and then shrugged one shoulder. "I was already pregnant with Lane when we got married. I was seventeen, and my dad... Well, if I was going to have a baby, I had to have a husband."

He leaned closer, the tilt of his mouth giving away his amusement. "You look pretty good for somebody who was seventeen in the 1940s."

Laura laughed, her hand going to his shoulder to push him away. Good Lord, he had strong shoulders. "Stop it. Did I mention my father was the pastor?"

"Ah. A preacher's daughter sneaking out for secret rides on her boyfriend's motorcycle."

"Yes, I was a cliché." She laughed, but memories chased the amusement away. "I couldn't sit down on my wedding day because all the yelling and threats wouldn't make me marry Joe, but the belt did."

"Oh, shit." Riley squeezed her hand, holding it tight. "I'm sorry, Laura. I wouldn't have joked about it if I knew."

She shook off the very old trauma and gave him a genuine smile. "No, it's fine. He's gone now, and I rarely think about it."

"When did he pass away?"

"Oh, he's not dead. Not that I know of, anyway. He moved to Las Vegas two years after Lane was born. He wanted to start one of those megachurches and become megarich, but he called two months in asking for a loan because he'd lost everything at the tables. I hung up on him, and he never called back."

"Good for you." He stroked her palm with his thumb. "I'm sorry, though. That's hard. What about your mother?"

"She mixed too many sleeping pills with too much alcohol when I was twelve." She heard his quick intake of breath and sighed. "And the answer to the question nobody asks is we don't know."

They'd never know, and Laura had long ago made

peace with that. Whether her mother had intended to die or not, she was gone and it was sad, so Laura mourned her without anger. And she'd had Ellen's mom to help her through the teen years, so she'd been okay. Right up until Joe Thompson turned her head with his pretty talk and sexy motorcycle.

"You don't have to talk about this. I didn't mean to bring you down."

She shook it off. "I hope you were getting around to inviting me out on a ride with you."

"That's where I was going with that, yes. I don't want it to be rushed, though, so I was thinking Saturday, if the long-range forecast holds and you don't have other plans."

She couldn't remember if she had plans without looking at her calendar, but she rarely had plans that couldn't be moved around. And she wanted to climb on the back of his Harley, wrap her arms around him and just ride out of town. She didn't even care where they went.

"I'd like that." She chuckled. "I never wore a helmet, though. Joe said the whole point was feeling the wind in your hair."

"I…don't share that philosophy, obviously. If it's a deal breaker, we can always go for a ride in the truck, but I won't take you out on the bike without a helmet."

"No!" she said quickly. "I didn't mean I *won't* wear one. I was trying to say that I've never owned one, so obviously I don't still have a helmet kicking around in the basement or the garage."

"They have a five-year shelf life, anyway. I have to run to my sister's after work tomorrow to watch her kids for a couple of hours, so I'll grab the helmets I keep in my parents' garage. Luckily, my mom and my sisters all have different-sized heads, so you'll have three sizes to choose from. One of them is bound to fit you."

"Do they have motorcycles, too, or do you just keep helmets for all the women in your life?"

"When I got the bike, they all wanted to go for a ride to see what it was like, but they needed helmets. So I gave my mom my credit card and told her they could all run to the Harley shop while I was at work and I'd take them out when I got home."

"That was generous of you."

"Yeah, well, I thought they'd buy one helmet, because I didn't know they all had different-sized heads when I said it. It took me four months to pay off that bill."

She laughed, and when she looked out over the yard, she realized people were watching them. It made her a little self-conscious, but she turned her attention back to Riley and tried to ignore everybody else.

"I'm looking forward to it now," she said. "I hope it's a nice day."

"I'll be with you," he said in a low voice. "So, rain or shine, it's going to be a nice day."

"You are so good with words," she said, and then she laughed again when he grinned and nudged her with his elbow. "Yes, you're good with other things, too."

"There's babysitting tomorrow, but maybe you can visit my place Wednesday night. And Thursday night. And Friday night. And—"

She laughed, cutting him off. "At least one of those nights. Or maybe two. But right now I'm going to go visit the potato salad again."

He stood, keeping her hand to help her up. "The pasta salad's better."

"I made that."

He gave her one of those naughty grins that turned her inside out. "I'm an even luckier man than I thought."

Chapter Seventeen

Town of Stonefield employment available: Seek-
ing a town administrator. Experience preferred.
Immediate start date. Salary is commensurate
with experience and will not include an expense
account. Interested candidates should submit
an application via the link on the town's web-
site or by mailing their résumé and a letter of
interest to the town hall.

        —Stonefield Gazette *Facebook Page*

Riley stood forward over the gas tank, with the bike
balanced between his legs, while Laura stepped onto
the back peg and worked her leg over. Once she'd sat
and scooted back to the backrest, he lowered himself to his seat.

She wiggled around a bit, getting a feel for it, which he'd expected. He wasn't in any hurry, and he liked the way the insides of her thighs rubbed against his hips. After a minute, she stopped moving and put her hands on his back. Then she leaned forward and wrapped her arms around his waist.

Finally, she moved back again, with her hands at his hips. "Okay."

He turned his head so she could hear him through the helmets. "You're sure?"

"I feel like I'm going to keep hitting your back with my helmet."

"You might, but it won't be hard enough to bother me. Don't worry about it." He reached down and put his hand on her knee. "And I know it's been a while since you've been on a bike, so if the leaning makes you nervous, it's easier if you relax your chest against my back and just move with me. Like a dance or... you know."

"I feel like I'm a more active participant in the *you know*."

"That you are, honey. Especially last night."

"Hey!"

Riley winced when he heard Lane yell, and he gave him a wave. "Sorry. Didn't know you were there."

Lane just shook his head. "Have fun, Mom. And you—be safe."

"Always."

Riley settled between Laura's thighs and let the bike start rolling. She didn't tense up or give him the Heimlich when he gave it throttle and leaned into the first corner, which was a relief. He wanted her to enjoy herself, and being terrified wasn't enjoyable unless you'd deliberately gone into a haunted house attraction.

Soon Stonefield was behind them, and the bike ate up the miles. If he was alone, he would have jumped on the highway, but he stuck to the back roads. They followed a river for a while, and sometimes he'd point things out to her. But the closer they got to the city, the more tense *he* got.

Riley hadn't told Laura what their first stop was, and she was probably confused, because the ride was definitely less scenic now.

Then he felt her stiffen against him when he slowed and leaned to turn into the car lot. The accident had been a headache for her in more ways than one, so he wasn't surprised she didn't want this to be a part of their day out, but he had his fingers crossed she was going to forgive him very soon.

He'd sent a text message to Derek, his brother-in-law's cousin, before they left the house, and he met them outside the office. Because he knew to look for it, Riley had spotted the car in the third parking space, and he smiled as he tapped her knee to tell her to climb off.

For a few seconds, he thought she was going to refuse to move, but then she climbed off the back and started unbuckling her helmet. He did the same

and avoided the glare she shot his way as he shook
Derek's hand.

"She's right there," Derek said, nodding his head in
the car's direction. "Here's the key, and there's a dealer
plate on it, if you want to take it for a test-drive."

"Thanks."

When he turned back to Laura, she had her arms
folded across her chest, and everything about her
body language said she was *not* pleased. He knew
her well enough to know that a man attempting to
manage her in any way was going to make her very
unhappy, but that wasn't what was happening. He
hoped.

"Just look at it," he said. "Please."

"Fine," she snapped, which any man knew meant
this is absolutely not fine.

He heard her gasp when he stopped in front of
the red Subaru, though, and when he turned back,
her hand was pressed to her mouth and her annoyance had vanished.

"It's my car," she said.

"A year newer and with a lot fewer miles, but
pretty close," he said. "And I confirmed that the in-
terior specs, including the cup holder and center console, did not change between the two model years."

"I've been looking for one online, but there weren't
any in New England."

"I asked Derek to keep an eye out for the year and
model. This one hasn't been listed yet, but they've
gone through it and it's in great shape. Lane put down

a small deposit to hold it until you have a chance to decide if you want it or not."

"You did this together?" Her eyes were filling up with tears.

"We know you loved your car." He shrugged, hoping to make her laugh. "And I'll need my truck back before it snows."

It worked, and the sound of her laughter filled the lot. Then she ran her hand over the car's hood. "It's even the same color."

"That's a happy coincidence." When he dangled the key in front of her, she smiled and nodded.

She hadn't even driven off the lot before she'd decided it was the one. They still went around the block so she could check the alignment and the brakes. She even put all four windows down so she could listen for any potential problems as she put the car through its paces.

Twenty minutes later, she had a signed agreement tucked away in his bike's saddlebag. The actual business of buying it and taking it home would wait for another day, but it was essentially hers and they could continue on with their adventure.

As he headed out of the city toward one of the scenic rides he favored, the fact he'd been able to make her so happy with such a simple thing made him feel about ten feet tall.

And when she leaned against him and put her arms around his waist, not because she was scared, but just because she liked it, he smiled to himself and wished the ride never had to end.

"Be honest with me," Riley said. "You're testing me with this show, aren't you?"

Laura laughed, which shook them both, since she was essentially sprawled on top of him on his couch. He'd stretched along the length and then pulled her down on top of him for a rather scorching kiss.

Then he'd scrolled through the channels until she'd mentioned she loved a particular show, and he'd stopped, tossing the remote onto the table.

"You don't have to watch this," she'd said.

"I don't care what we watch. And if you like it, it can't be that bad."

He'd snorted so many times while watching the young couple tour homes in hopes of finding their dream house, she was afraid he'd damage his sinuses. But he never reached for the remote, so that was a point in his favor.

"That guy doesn't look old enough to shave," he grumbled. "And he's a canine massage therapist, and his wife is a preschool teacher. How do they have a two-million-dollar budget?"

"That's why it's such a fun show."

"Sure. I love watching this after I've worked my ass off all day to come home to my one-bedroom apartment above a funeral home's hearse garage."

"But it's a cheery color." She gestured to his bright

yellow walls, which made him laugh. "And I told you we don't have to watch it."

"Nope. I'm watching this until I figure out what *midcentury modern* means. Also *shiplap*. What the hell is shiplap?"

Laura decided to put him out of his misery. She stretched to get the remote and turned the TV off, and then she fished in the tote she'd dropped on the floor for the book he'd been reading to her after the accident.

She dropped it on his chest. "We have to finish reading this book, anyway. It's seriously overdue."

"Why didn't you renew it? You can even do it online."

"I like going to the library in person." Then a guilty flush heated her cheeks. "And there's a waiting list, so Callan said I couldn't renew it. I left with it because there was nothing he could really do to stop me."

"You didn't."

"I'm not giving it back until you've read the rest to me. But then Molly stopped by, claiming she wanted to see Becca, but I caught her snooping through the books on my side table."

His eyes widened. "Wait. The librarian sent his fiancée to steal the library book back from your house?"

"She's next on the waiting list." She shrugged. "I'm not sure how involved he was in the attempted book heist."

He laughed. "I love this town. My sister told me I was going to be so bored living in Stonefield, but she really has no idea."

"Well, she probably also didn't guess you'd get involved in a torrid affair with your boss's mother."

He chuckled. "No, I'm pretty sure none of them had that on their 'Riley in a small town' bingo card. I do like the word *torrid*, though."

"I'm not even sure what it means," she confessed. "I just know affairs always seem to be torrid."

"I want to put a pin in torrid for a second. I definitely want to circle back to that." He cleared his throat. "But first, speaking of my family…"

Uh-oh. Laura tried not to tense up, but if he was about to share *their* opinions on his relationship with her, she wasn't sure she wanted to hear it.

"You know how I went to Evie's birthday barbecue with you?" He grinned when she nodded. "We're having a birthday barbecue for my mother next week. I'd really like for you to go with me."

Good Lord, he wanted to take her home to meet his parents.

She had no idea how she felt about that. She liked that he was close with his family. She'd heard him talking to the kids on the phone, as well as his parents. His sisters texted him often, and he'd shown her pictures of his nieces and nephews.

On some level, she'd known she'd meet them eventually. Maybe they'd run into his parents or one of his sisters at the big grocery store in the city.

Or at the home improvement warehouse. Or some-where—anywhere but at their home in a "here's my girlfriend" kind of way.

"You're not saying anything." He dipped his head so he could see her eyes. "If you don't want to, it's cool. It was just a thought."

No, it wasn't. He loved his family and he wanted them to meet her. It mattered to him, so it mattered to her.

"Of course I'll go," she said quickly. "I was just thinking about what's going on next week. You'll have to text me the details tomorrow so I'll remember to tell Lane and Evie I won't be around."

The smile he gave her was a sweet reward, and then his hand cupped the back of her neck as he drew her in for a kiss. The kiss deepened, and he slid his other hand up her back, under her shirt.

When she tugged up on the hem of his T-shirt, wanting it out of the way of that button on his jeans, the book slid to the floor and neither of them cared.

It wasn't easy getting their clothes off on the couch, especially since they kept stopping to kiss or to laugh when he couldn't get his foot free of the leg of his jeans and almost fell on the floor.

She had a condom in her bag, which was within reach, so they didn't have to get up. Instead, he took advantage of her stretching to grab the strap to run his hands up her side and close his mouth over her nipple. Her back arched and it was almost her turn to fall on the floor, but he held her tight—still suck-

ing gently on her taut nipples—so she could strad-
dle his lap.

She nipped at his jaw as she lifted herself enough
so he could roll the condom on, and then she lowered
herself. Teasing him because she loved the way he
groaned deep in his throat, she pushed down onto
him slowly, in tiny strokes, until he couldn't take it
anymore and his hips thrust upward.

Laura gasped as he filled her, and his mouth went
to her breasts. His hands were cupping her ass, urging her to ride him, and she let him set the pace. Her
fingers gripped his shoulders, and she threw her head
back, loving the feel of his strong body.

She could tell by Riley's breathing he was close,
and he reached down to stroke her clit until her orgasm rocked her body. He thrust upward, hard and
fast, his fingertips digging almost painfully into her
hips until he shuddered and groaned her name.

When they'd caught their breath, she was left feeling lazy and languid. Draped across him, she soaked
in the heat of his body and tried not to actually purr
while he stroked her hair.

"If you let me run to the bathroom for a minute,
I'll read the end of that book to you. I was so distracted by who the murderer is, I could barely keep
that erection going."

She laughed and slapped his chest because he was
totally lying. But then she forced herself to get up so
he could go to the bathroom. Then she took a turn,

and when she came out, he was standing in the middle of the room, frowning at his phone.

"What's the matter?" she asked. "Did you get a text from somebody?"

"No, I looked up what shiplap is." He looked up at her, shaking his head. "People are putting this in their living rooms?"

Chapter Eighteen

The totals for the Badges For Backpacks Drive are in, and the winner is Stonefield Police Department by a pencil! The supplies that were donated by our very generous community are being distributed just in time for school to start next week. With slightly fewer donations taken in, the members of the Stonefield Fire Department will be washing and waxing the police vehicles. Police Chief Bordeaux says the time will be posted on the website and the public is invited to watch. Fire Chief Nelson promises to pull out all the stops for the Christmas toy drive. Get to donation shopping, Stonefield!

—Stonefield Gazette *Facebook Page*

When Riley walked out of the garage a little before midmorning and almost ran into Bruce Fletcher, he was surprised, to say the least. Bruce and his crew didn't spend a lot of time at the garage, and certainly never during the day. And Bruce was scowling more than usual.

"Anything wrong?" Riley asked, hoping the guy wasn't sick, as his brain got a head start on solving the problem. Case would have to cover for Bruce, which meant either rearranging his own schedule, or getting Lane in from the brewery to cover.

"My brother's car got towed from in front of his shop, and he needs a ride to get it back."

Okay. Not sick, which was a relief. "Can't he walk to the police station from there?"

"Yup." Bruce nodded. "But when Vinnie has to tow a vehicle on the police chief's say-so, he has to take it to his place and put it inside the fence, and that's one hell of a walk. But I came back because I've got a meeting with the guy from the power company."

"I finished the first thing on my list, and the crew is on a job they don't need me for. I just wrote up an estimate, and I don't have a set appointment time for my second job, so I can pick him up and give him a ride."

Bruce looked surprised. "You don't mind?"

"Of course not. It'll be a lot easier for me to do

than for you to reschedule a meeting with the power company."

"I appreciate it. I'd ask my wife, but the baby has an ear infection, and my daughter just turned two, and I guess that birthday kicks off the 'possessed by a loud, destructive demon phase,' so when I say asking her for a favor is the last resort, I mean it."

"That phase is why I'm thankful I'm just the uncle and I can go home," Riley said. "I'll head over to his shop now."

"He was on his way to the police station when I talked to him, and he said Margaret's in a mood, so the paperwork might take a while."

"Not a problem. Give him my number and tell him I'll be there when he's ready."

A half hour later, John Fletcher climbed into the passenger side of Riley's truck and introduced himself. "I really appreciate this."

"No problem. If Bruce hadn't had to meet with the power company, he would have come himself. Did you get an address to the impound lot?"

"Yeah. I put it into my phone, and we're heading east out of town," he said. Riley put the truck in gear, but he left his foot on the brake because John swore under his breath. Then he shook his head. "You've got to be kidding me."

"What's wrong?" Riley asked, and then he followed the guy's gaze to the Perkin' Up Café cup in his center console. "That's from yesterday. Did you want to stop for a coffee?"

"Absolutely not." He said it with so much feroc-
ity, Riley gave him a sideways look.

"Okay. Not a fan of coffee. Noted."

"No, I'm…" John stopped and scrubbed his face
over his hands with a chuckle. "I'm sorry. Did you
know she's the one who had my car towed?"

"Chelsea?" Since there was nothing actually wrong,
Riley pulled out of the police department's lot and
headed east. "That doesn't sound like her. She's so
sweet and she gets along with everybody."

John snorted. "Except me."

"So maybe the problem is you," Riley said. He
didn't know this guy—Bruce's brother or not—but
he'd gotten to know Chelsea, and if she didn't like
this guy, she had a good reason.

He expected John to be offended, but he surprised
him by nodding. "Probably a little bit me. I told her
coffee is disgusting."

"Coffee in general, or *her* coffee in particular?"

"I was talking about coffee in general, but it's
possible she didn't take it that way. I might also have
said something about jacking up the price because
the milk is foamy. She got angry and walked away
before I realized that was probably an insulting thing
to say to a woman who owned a coffee shop and
walked it back." He pointed to a sign in the distance.
"Turn right at that sign."

After he dropped John at the impound lot and
had stuck around for a confirmation he'd be getting
his car back, Riley headed back toward town. On a

whim, he used his phone's hands-free feature to call Laura. She answered on the second ring.

"Hey, guess what I'm doing right now," she said by way of greeting.

"How many guesses do I get? Does it involve being naked? Batteries?"

Her laughter echoed through his truck. "You're so bad. And no. I'm driving my new car and talking to you through the speakers."

They'd picked it up yesterday afternoon, and though he hadn't been able to go with her, she'd sent him a text from the lot thanking him again for finding it. He wasn't sure who had shown her how to use the hands-free function, which was one of the major changes between the model she'd had and the new car, but he was glad she had it.

"Where are you headed?" he asked.

"I'm going to see Ellen, but I'm on my way to the café first for some caffeine. Somebody kept me up too late texting me dirty things."

He grinned, flipping his turn signal on because the GPS was telling him it was time to turn. "Speaking of the café, guess what I was just doing."

"Did it involve being naked?"

"That would have been weird. I just gave John Fletcher a ride to the impound lot to pick up his car because Chelsea had it towed and Bruce was busy."

"You're kidding. That doesn't sound like Chelsea at all."

"That's what I said, but he's definitely not a fan."

"She's definitely not a fan of him, either. But having his car towed is next level."

"Oh, damn, I'm here already. I thought this job was farther away." He put the truck in Park. "I have to run, but call me later and fill me in if you hear any more about it."

"I will. Be safe, and I'll talk to you soon."

After he disconnected the call, Riley shut off the truck and grabbed the clipboard with the contract he needed the customer to sign. And as he walked to the door, he caught himself whistling, which he rarely did.

It was really nice to have somebody to check in with—somebody who cared about his day.

There was one customer in the café when Laura arrived—a young woman with AirPods in who was moving her head as though listening to music, swiping through her phone with one hand and holding a beverage in the other. It was close enough to being alone with Chelsea.

"I heard a rumor you got John Fletcher's car towed this morning," she said once she had her latte in hand.

Chelsea groaned and covered her face with her hands for a moment. Her cheeks were red when she dropped them again. "I didn't know they'd tow it."

"But you did call the police on him?"

"I thought they'd make him move it and he'd be annoyed." She sighed, her body slumping so her hip rested against the counter. "He complained to me about trash in front of his door the other day. It wasn't even one of my cups, Laura. So this morning, he parked crooked because the truck on the other side was crooked. The back of his car ended up over the line into one of my spots—you know, the two the town made fifteen-minute parking only, so I'd almost always have parking—and after an hour, I called Margaret and complained."

Margaret ran the desk at the police station. "And they towed it?"

Chelsea nodded, her face still flushed with guilt. "I called her again after they left, and she said the chief's super touchy about the parking because they did that survey last year about making the spots bigger because vehicles have gotten bigger, but people didn't want to add repainting all the lines to the budget. So they voted against fixing the parking but are still complaining about the parking."

"I guess if you wanted to annoy John Fletcher, you certainly succeeded."

Chelsea pressed her lips together, but the lift at the corners gave her away. "I certainly did. But I didn't mean to annoy him *that* much."

"I doubt it'll improve his mood any."

"How did you find out?"

"He called Bruce for a ride to pick up his car, but he had a meeting with the power company and Riley's job wasn't a set time, so he went and got him."

"Ouch. So I managed to annoy multiple people with one phone call."

"I don't know about anybody else, but Riley—who was the one who did the favor—wasn't annoyed at all. Did you at least get to see John's face when he realized his car was gone?"

"I didn't see his expression when he realized it was gone, but he did turn and look at me through the window. Everybody will be glad to know John Fletcher doesn't have the power to set people on fire with his eyes, no matter how hard he tries."

Laura laughed, but her amusement faded as the reality of Chelsea's situation sank in. "Are you worried about him at all, though? Bruce might be a great guy, but John is new to town. None of us really know him."

"I don't think he's dangerous or anything. And I have cameras, so if he tries to damage the shop, he'll have to fix it and the landlord would probably evict him. I think I'll apologize, though. If I'd known the chief was in a mood and would have it towed, I never would have called."

"That'll be an interesting conversation. 'I was only trying to annoy you a little bit, so I'm sorry I annoyed you a lot.'"

Chelsea laughed. "That's probably what I'll end up saying. Where are you off to now?"

"I'm going to stop by the Sutton house and see Ellen. We've both been so busy, it feels like I've hardly seen her."

"I'm sure Riley's keeping you pretty busy these days." The innuendo was thick, and Laura chuckled, but her mind was hung up on what she'd said. *It feels like I've hardly seen her.*

Had she been neglecting her friendship with Ellen?

She wasn't sure the answer was no. The time she'd spent with Riley was time she probably would have spent with her best friend. Over the last week or two, there were probably more text messages in her conversation thread with Riley than the one with Ellen. And if she wasn't talking to him, she was thinking about him.

When Laura arrived at the Sutton house, she knocked on the door and then waited for a few seconds before letting herself in. There was a time she'd never knocked at all, but once Irish moved in, she'd started giving them a token warning somebody was about to walk in.

"I'm in the kitchen," Ellen called. When Laura entered, she found her friend refilling the sugar bowl and smiled. "You look happy today. I take it the fling with your young man is going well."

The way she said it set Laura's teeth on edge. "His name is Riley, not *my young man*, and I don't know if it's a fling. It might be more."

Ellen froze for a few seconds, her good humor fading. "Oh. I didn't realize it might be serious."

Even though she'd come over here feeling guilty that she'd been neglecting her friendship a little, the look on Ellen's face was dismaying. "I thought you'd be happier for me."

Ellen closed the sugar bowl with a snap of glass

that made Laura wince. Then she carried the big plastic container of sugar back to the pantry. "Of course I'm happy for you. Go, have fun. I have plenty of things to keep me busy. Like refilling sugar bowls and looking for Eli's phone cord."

"Please don't be like this," Laura said.

The pleading tone of her voice seemed to deflate Ellen's temper, and she dropped into a chair. "I'm sorry. I really am happy for you. I just thought we were going to have fun adventures together. Lucy and Lucy," she said with a sad smile.

"We'll *always* be Lucy and Lucy. You know that. And we can still have fun adventures."

"I don't want to be a third wheel. I can just imagine one of you saying, 'I guess we should ask Ellen if she wants to go,' and then silently resenting me for crashing your date night."

"Ellen!" Shock kept her from saying anything else for a long moment, and all she could do was shake her head.

"It's true," Ellen said.

"Really?" The anger that rose up in Laura surprised her. "Is that how you and David felt after Joe died? Did you say to each other, 'I guess we should ask Laura if she wants to go,' and then silently resent me?"

Ellen drew back, looking as startled as if Laura had actually slapped her. "Of course not! We both loved spending time with you. How can you even think that?"

"Do you hear yourself? You literally just said if you went out with Riley and me, that you'd be the third wheel we didn't want. How can I *not* think it's because that's what I was to you and David?"

"You were never a third wheel. And I know you wouldn't see me that way." A tear slipped over Ellen's cheek. "I don't know what's wrong with me. I'm just feeling blue, I guess. But I want you to be happy. I really do."

"I know. I think I'm in a mood, too. And I have so much to do today." She'd come to spend some time with Ellen, but maybe they both needed a little space to work through their first spat in so many years, Laura couldn't even remember the last one. They'd even gotten through their kids divorcing without losing each other. "I just stopped to say hi, but I need to get back to the office."

"I'm glad you stopped by, even though I guess I'm not great company today. There have been so many changes over the last few years and sometimes it's a lot."

"We all have those days, but what's not ever going to change is our friendship, Ellen." Her friend *almost* believed her. She wanted to, but Laura could see a little skepticism lurking in Ellen's eyes. "What we need is a trip to the yarn store soon."

But as she drove away, Laura wasn't making a mental list of colorways and yarn weights she wanted. All she could think about was her relationship with

Riley on one side of the scale and her friendship with Ellen on the other.

It wasn't fair, and she drove home too fast with the radio too loud.

Chapter Nineteen

*Heads up, library patrons! According to Mr.
Avery, overdue fines will be doubled for any
book that has a waiting list, and it goes into
effect at the end of next month. His reason?
"I can't provide materials to the residents of
Stonefield if other residents won't bring them
back. If a patron puts their name on a waiting
list for a book, they're excited to read it. I want
to put that book in their hands, which means
we need an incentive for everybody to return
their books on time."*
—Stonefield Gazette *Facebook Post*

Riley pulled his truck into his parents' driveway,
squeezing half onto the lawn next to his sister's SUV.

He'd wanted to bring the bike, but there was a slight chance of rain. Plus, Laura said she didn't want to meet his entire family with helmet hair, so the truck it was.

"I can't believe I let you talk me into this," she said for the eighth or ninth time since they left Stonefield.

"I didn't talk you into it," he told her, reaching over to take her hand. "I invited you. And I went to your family's birthday barbecue, remember?"

"Yes, I do remember. But you already knew everybody, so it's not exactly the same thing."

"Good point. But like I said, my dad's very relaxed. My sisters have their hands full with kids and don't really care what I'm doing as long as I'm happy doing it. And my mom?" He smiled at her. "I'm her boy. I think you know what that means. She has some anxiety. But she's also nice and funny and smart, so I think once the introductions are out of the way, you'll get along well."

She blew out a breath and gave him a sharp nod. "Fine."

It wasn't quite the enthusiasm he'd been hoping for, but at least she got out of the truck. And she let him hold her hand as he led her around the house to the backyard. Riley knew under other circumstances, meeting new people wouldn't faze her at all. She was a confident, social woman. But she knew how much his family meant to him, so she was probably concerned that if they didn't like her, it was going to be a problem for Riley.

When his niece yelled "Uncle Riley!" all the adults stopped talking and turned to look.

And because the kids were on the far side of the yard and it took them a minute to get to him, he saw the disbelief on his mom's face. And it was followed by dismay.

He was saved from Laura seeing it because she was focused on three kids running toward them. The littlest two were also making their way over, though the youngest—eighteen months old—would probably fall on her butt several times before she got there.

Tara greeted them first, and then Riley introduced Laura to each of them. As he'd expected, his dad didn't seem to notice that his son's girlfriend looked older than him. His sisters communicated their surprise to each other with facial expressions when Laura had her back to them. But his mother had that pinched look around her mouth that already had him regretting the whole thing.

Luckily, Laura relaxed quickly and was her wonderful and gracious self. His brothers-in-law were just finishing up at the grill when they arrived, so eating bumped that awkward period of "getting to know you" questions. He wasn't sad about that.

"So what do you do for work, Laura?" his mother asked after she'd finished eating.

"I do the books and manage the office for the tree service."

"The tree service Riley works for?" Tammy asked,

and then she looked at her brother in surprise. "You're dating your boss?"

Riley chuckled. "Even better. I'm dating my boss's mother."

His sisters laughed, but his mother stiffened as though she'd been given an electrical shock under the table. She waited a couple of minutes so it wouldn't be obvious, but then she stood.

"Riley, can you help me carry the desserts out?"

"You're not supposed to carry your own birthday cake, Mom," Tara said.

"And that's why I asked Riley to come with me."

He was probably about to get an earful, but he didn't let his smile slip as he turned to Laura. Under the table, he squeezed her hand. "I'll be right back."

"We have a few favorite authors in common," his dad said. "She'll be just fine talking books with me for a few minutes."

"Minutes?" He laughed. "Hours is more like it."

Then he kissed the back of Laura's hand and got up from the picnic table to follow his mom into the house. She was walking fast, which wasn't a good sign, and she already had the birthday cake and a tray of cookies on the counter.

"She's your boss's *mother*?" Her hands were on her hips.

"I thought I told you that. You asked where we met."

"And you said she works for the tree service. You did not mention she gave birth to the owner."

"That's a little melodramatic. And if he doesn't have a problem with it—which he doesn't, by the way—I don't see why anybody else should."

Recognizing the conversational dead end, she detoured. "You told me she's your age."

"I said she's *around* my age, and she is." He shrugged. "Roughly."

"In the same way vodka is *around* the same as French fries because they're both from potatoes," she said, and he shook his head. That didn't even make sense. "I was so excited you were finally bringing a girlfriend home to meet us. I thought it was a sign you're finally ready to settle down and give me some grandchildren."

"Mom, you have *five* grandchildren. Those kids destroying your backyard right now are your grandchildren."

She rolled her eyes. "Yes, I am aware of that. But it would be nice if my *son* would give me a grandson with the McLaughlin last name."

"You can't be serious, Mom." When he saw that she was, he laughed. "That's one of the most ridiculous things I've ever heard."

"What's ridiculous about it? Your father only has sisters and you only have sisters. There won't be any more McLaughlins if you don't have a baby."

"I'm not having this conversation with you. I wanted you to meet Laura because I thought you'd like her, but we can leave."

Kris put her hand on his arm. "Don't leave. I *do*

like her. It's not about whether or not I like her, Riley. I just wasn't expecting to…have so much in common with your new girlfriend."

He'd come to a conversational crossroads—he could get angry and walk out or he could let the jab go. He was leaning toward leaving and finishing the conversation with his mother once he'd calmed down and she'd had some time to come to terms with his new relationship. But he knew that would be awkward for Laura, and she'd feel bad if she thought she was the cause of an argument between him and his family.

"We're here to celebrate your birthday, Mom. Let's go do that."

"I didn't mean to ruin my special day for you."

"Don't." His voice was low, but he saw the way her jaw tightened. "If you want to sulk and be passive-aggressive, I'm going to leave. But if you want to let this go and have a good time and eat some cake together, I would love to do that."

"I'm sorry, honey. Let's have cake."

She managed to keep a smile on her face for the rest of the party, but it was brittle and he could only hope Laura didn't notice. And as soon as the festivities were over and the party had slid into "just sitting around talking" mode, he hugged the kids, kissed his mother's cheek and got Laura out of there.

Laura wasn't sure what had happened between Riley and his mother in the kitchen, but his mood definitely changed while he was inside. The change was subtle—the set of his shoulders and less sparkle in his eyes—but it was there.

And based on the brittleness in Kris's trying-too-hard smile, Laura was afraid whatever was said, it was said about her. If they'd met at a coffee shop or struck up a conversation in a grocery store line, she and Kris would probably get along great. Kris probably saw that and mentally put her in a "peer" column, which meant Laura had no business dating her son.

She was wrong, of course. Laura wasn't Kris's age. And Riley was definitely an adult, capable of making his own decisions. But on the flip side, she didn't want to come between them in any way.

But Riley didn't say anything, so she didn't, either. He was probably hoping she hadn't noticed, which was laughable because Kris wasn't as subtle as she thought she was, but Laura could pretend if it meant not getting into a heavy discussion with a man about his mother. That almost never ended well.

Since they didn't have to work tomorrow, she'd packed an overnight bag and was going to spend the night at Riley's place. Becca was six months old now, and Laura had been consciously stepping back from a constant "Nana's on duty" role. She loved the kids and she loved her granddaughter, but it would be too easy for Lane and Evie to start assuming she was always around. She wanted to start setting subtle boundaries now to save having to draw hard lines later.

They might think it was because of Riley, but

mostly it was about her being determined to not be taken for granted again. She'd been there, done that, and it was something she was always conscious of. Anything she did was because she wanted to do it, not because it was expected of her.

Two hours later, when they were curled up on the couch in their comfy, TV-watching sweats—which she considered a pretty substantial relationship milestone—Riley picked up the remote and muted the sound.

"You're a million miles away. Let's talk about it." She started to deny it, but he shook his head. "You didn't laugh at that joke, and it was funny."

"Did you know everybody thinks we're just having a fling?"

"I don't really care what other people label it."

"Really?" she challenged. "You don't care at all how Kris feels about it?"

He winced, and she knew she'd hit a soft spot. "I'm sorry about today. She was just…surprised. And part of that is she refuses to recognize I'm as old as I am, you know."

Laura's lips twitched, almost smiling, because she knew how that felt. "But she might be the first person who hasn't jumped to the conclusion this is a fling, and that I'm a cougar and you're my prey or whatever. And that's why it upset her."

"I don't understand why that should upset her. And I don't really care, to be honest. Why is this even a conversation *anybody* is having?"

"I'm a grandmother, Riley."

"I know. I've seen you with your granddaughter. You light up when you see her and it's beautiful. *You're* beautiful."

She refused to let his pretty words throw her off track. "When I say I'm a grandmother, it's not about whether or not I think I'm attractive or sexy or whatever."

"Which you are."

As much as she loved the words coming out of his mouth, it wasn't making what she needed to say any easier. "It's about the phase of life I'm in, Riley. My life is about my granddaughter and my son and this business. Going to yard sales with Ellen."

"And you think there's no room in there for me?"

"There is room for you," she said quietly. She didn't know how to say the rest of it, but she had to just spit it out because it had to be said. "But only for you. I'm not...I'm not in the same phase of life as you."

He leaned back, his gaze roaming over her face as though looking for something. She tried to keep her expression as neutral as possible, so he couldn't see how painful it was for her to imagine him moving on with another woman. But it was probably the right thing for him to do, even if it made her chest ache.

"The same phase of life," he said slowly, as if the words were puzzle pieces he was turning around in his mind, trying to figure out how they fit into the bigger picture.

"I'm not having another child," she said bluntly, and once she got that out, the rest was easier. "Even though it's possible at my age nowadays, I don't *want* to."

"Ah." He nodded, the corner of his mouth lifting into an almost smile. "Maybe it was wrong of me, but I just assumed you wouldn't't."

"Oh."

"When I look at you, Laura, I see a beautiful woman who's living a very full life and loving her family—especially her gorgeous, very loud and sometimes smelly granddaughter—and who doesn't need anything or anybody else to make her happy." He put his hand on her knee, his thumb stroking her skin through the soft cotton. "I find that woman superhot and amazing, and I'm very, *very* happy to be a part of her life. I don't need more than what we have."

The man always knew the right thing to say. And it would be easy to accept what he said—to let her fears go—but with every day that passed, she fell more in love with Riley.

"What about five years from now? What about family events where Case, Lane and Irish have their little ones? And probably Callan at some point, since he and Molly are getting married. How will you not wish you had a baby, too?"

"I'll hold one of theirs for a bit. I'm pretty sure they won't mind, and there's nothing like wrangling a pack of babies to make you question whether you want any."

His hand had left her knee and was running up and down her thigh. She swatted it away. "You're not distracting me right now."

He grinned and put his hands back in his own lap. "Look. I have five nieces and nephews. You have a baby granddaughter, and I know Lane wants at least one more. Plus the Sutton kids. We have an entire gaggle of kids in our lives."

She laughed. "A gaggle? Isn't that geese?"

"Probably, but it felt like a good word. They run around squawking and flapping, they poop everywhere and they try to steal my fries."

"That's fair."

"Now, I'm going to rewind this so you can hear the joke, and when this show is over, I'm going to take you to bed and prove just how sexy I think you are."

She laughed, and she tried to pay attention to the sitcom they'd landed on earlier, but his words had unsettled her because they circled away from their problems and back to the one thing that *wasn't* complicated about their relationship.

Laura didn't need Riley to prove he thought she was sexy. She'd read that in his eyes from the first day they'd met. What she needed to know was that the weight of disappointing the ones they loved wasn't going to crush them.

Chapter Twenty

A reminder from our police chief: "After the motion to add repainting the parking lines downtown to the annual budget was shot down, there's a new process for parking complaints. Write out your complaint on a piece of paper. Ball it up. Then set it on fire." We reached out to our fire chief for a follow-up: "No. Don't set balls of paper on fire. People complain enough about the parking to make that a fire hazard. Just throw the complaints in the garbage." The Board of Selectmen have no comment.
—Stonefield Gazette *Facebook Page*

By Tuesday afternoon, Riley was out of ideas on how to fix his relationship with Laura. For one thing, he couldn't identify exactly what had gone wrong. Sure, his mom had been kind of a jerk, but Laura wasn't going to let a little attitude problem from another woman keep her from living her life the way she wanted.

She'd been okay when they first woke up on Sunday morning. They'd gone to the diner for breakfast and she'd been a little quiet, but he'd kept her up a little late. But there was a subtle distance from him he didn't like, as though she'd withdrawn some small part of herself.

And he hadn't seen her at all since he dropped her at her house on Sunday evening. She'd kissed him goodbye, gone inside and been busy ever since. He'd called her last night when he got home and they'd talked for a little while, but she hadn't been herself.

And he wanted to know why. And he was going to cheat if he had to. Once the other guys were gone, he pulled out his phone and sent her a text message.

I think there's a problem with the check I got today. I don't know if it's valid.

It was a big check, so it didn't take long for her to respond. If you bring it up, I can look at it.

When he walked into the office, he could see at a glance she wasn't herself. She looked exhausted, as if she hadn't been sleeping. And while there was a possibility Becca had an ear infection or was teething or something and had been keeping the entire household up, he couldn't shake the feeling it was because of him.

He handed her the check. "There's nothing wrong with it. I just needed a way to see you because I think you've been dodging me."

"I'm not dodging you. I just…"

"What's going on, Laura? Is this because of my mom?"

"No." She sighed. "But also yes? And Ellen. She's been struggling because we were going to be widows together and have adventures. Maybe go on a cruise."

He felt a flash of anger, which he did his best to tamp down. "And she expects you to be alone for the entire rest of your life so you can go on a cruise and hang out with her?"

"Don't make it sound like that." She wiped her hand over her face. "When I'm with you, I'm happier than I ever thought it was possible to be."

"I'd feel better about that if you didn't look so sad while saying it."

"But our relationship is coming between us and our families."

His body felt cold, and there was a trembling deep inside that he knew she couldn't see, but he felt it. This couldn't be happening. "I feel like you're the only person who thinks that."

"But I'm not. The people who are realizing it's *not* a fling aren't handling it well. And I absolutely will not be a source of conflict between you and your mother."

"She's wrong to—"

"No, she's not. That's the problem. She's right. You deserve everything life has to offer, including a wife and kids. And maybe you think you'll be okay without them, but I'm not going to take that away from you."

"How about you let *me* decide what I want?"

He was about to tell her exactly what he wanted—the woman he was completely and irreversibly in love with—when she shook her head.

"The longer this goes on, the harder it will be for everybody. I just have a different life than what you should be living, and you're going to wake up one day and realize it. And we might be…invested then. And it'll hurt more and be messy, and that *would* be an issue between you and Lane—with the tree service."

And we might be…invested then.

Which meant she wasn't invested now. Clearly Laura was the one who wasn't happy their fling might be something more, and now she was going to bail. And she thought it wasn't going to hurt because they weren't invested.

She was wrong.

But he didn't know what else to say. He'd shown her every day how he felt about her. If that wasn't enough to show her he was invested as hell, he didn't know what else he could do.

"You're really doing this?" he asked, his voice so rough it was barely more than a whisper.

"It's the best thing for everybody."

"It's not the best thing for me," he said, and then he turned around and walked out of the house.

He didn't stop back at the garage and say goodbye to anybody. His heart was cracked wide open in his chest and he didn't want to talk to anybody. He sure as hell didn't want to talk to Lane or Case.

All he wanted to do was lock himself in his apartment and try to figure out how the best thing in his life had gone so wrong, so fast.

Doing the right thing could be so incredibly painful. Laura sat at the kitchen table the next morning, staring at her cold coffee and wishing she could work up the energy to go do something. She didn't even know what. Just something other than sitting in her gloomy kitchen on a dreary day, not caring about anything going on around her.

She missed Riley. She was miserable to the point she didn't even care about drinking her coffee, which was unlike her, to say the least.

"Mom?" She hadn't even noticed Lane walking into the kitchen. "Are you sick?"

Yes, she was. She was sick and tired of being alone while surrounded by friends and family. "No."

"Okay. You're still in your pajamas, and I can see by the cream that your coffee is cold, which never happens."

"Is there some reason I should have gotten dressed?"

He frowned, shaking his head. "I guess not. But

it's two o'clock and… I don't know. It's just not like you."

"I'm going to get dressed in a little bit, since I'm going with Ellen to the garden club meeting tonight." And Ellen would be happy because she had her co-Lucy back.

And Kris McLaughlin would be happy because her son was free to find a woman who'd marry him and give him little McLaughlin boys. The people in this town could go back to complaining about parking and gossiping about each other instead of talking about her. Really, it would work out better for everybody.

Maybe not for her, but at least everybody else would be happy.

Anger pushed through the numbness, making her hands curl into fists. "I'm going to call Daphne Fisk and ask her to find me a little place somewhere."

"What?" Shock made Lane's body turn rigid, and she felt some of it herself.

The words had fallen out of her without conscious thought, but as soon as they left her mouth, they felt right. Lane and Evie were rebuilding their life together, and maybe having her in the house for Becca made it a little easier, but they needed their space and privacy. And she didn't want to live here anymore.

"I'll still come during the day to work in the office. And of course I'll be here for Becca when you need me, but it's time for me to have my own space. I want a place of my own that I chose for myself, and that makes me happy."

"This is your home," he said in a tight voice. "I'm not pushing you out of it. Evie and I can be the ones to find a little place somewhere."

"I appreciate that, but you're not listening to me. I need you to *hear* me." She waited until he focused on her, his brow furrowed, before she continued. "You know your dad inherited this property from his parents. It was your grandfather's house and then your father's house, and now it's your house."

"No, it's not. It's been *your* house since you married Dad and—"

"Lane! I hate this house."

His eyes widened, and his mouth opened and closed a couple of times before a single word came out. "Oh."

She hadn't meant to yell it out like that. "I'm sorry. I know you love this house, but I don't."

"It's a nice house, though."

"It's a gorgeous house, but I've hated it since I moved in when I was seventeen and pregnant with you. Old houses like these, they have small rooms and hallways, and the windows are small enough so you have to have a light on during the day. I want a wide-open space with huge windows that fill it with natural light. I want a breakfast nook and a big, walk-in shower. I just want…space and light. I don't know how to explain it."

"You don't have to, Mom. I just never realized you're unhappy here and that's on me."

"No." She pointed a finger at him, giving him her

stern Mom look. "I'm not *unhappy* here. The house doesn't suit me, but I've been very happy living here with you, and I can't even tell you how much joy being here with Evie and Becca has given me. There's a big difference between craving natural light and an open-concept floor plan, and being unhappy."

He waved a hand at her. "You don't look happy."

"This has nothing to do with you or this house." She pushed back from the table and walked to the sink to dump out the cold coffee.

When she turned back, Lane was giving her a speculative look. "Is it Riley?"

"It was too complicated. I cut him loose."

"Mom, I—"

She walked out of the kitchen and down the hall to her room. She didn't want to hear it. And she certainly didn't want to talk about it—not with her son or anybody else. Losing Riley was going to be a private hurt she would tuck away in her heart and probably never let go of.

She showered, running the water extra hot in an effort to revitalize her skin. Then she twisted her towel-dried hair up in a scrunchie, knowing it would be a mess later and not caring. After dressing in a long T-shirt over leggings, she added a cardigan because the heat of the shower was already seeping away, leaving a chill in its wake.

When she pulled into the Suttons' driveway, she could hear the cheerful, welcoming sounds coming from the taproom in the converted carriage house next door and, for the first time, wished they had the full liquor license so they could sell hard liquor. Drinking enough beer to obliterate thoughts of Riley would make her some kind of sick, if she could even drink that much of it.

Instead, she climbed the porch steps, knocked and then let herself in. Irish was walking through the living room, Leeza cradled in his arm, and for a few seconds, the joy of seeing the cowboy gazing adoringly at his infant daughter penetrated the dark cloud.

That was how she would get through this, she told herself. Friends and family. The babies. She'd pretend to be okay, focus on them, and someday it wouldn't be a lie anymore.

"Hey, Laura. Ellen's in the kitchen, but you probably already guessed that." His smile slipped as he really looked at her. "Are you okay?"

"I'm fine." And she still didn't want to talk about it. "I should go find Ellen or we'll be late."

Ellen did an actual double take when Laura walked into the kitchen. "Honey, what's wrong?"

Laura stood still, looking at her best friend in the world. And she didn't throw herself into her arms, sobbing. She didn't confess she'd broken her own heart into a million pieces. She forced a smile on her face. "I'm fine."

"The hell you are." Ellen pulled out a chair and pointed to the seat. "Sit."

"We'll be late to the garden club meeting."

"Screw the garden club. You're going to tell me what happened."

Even though Laura still hadn't sat, Ellen put the kettle on, and she knew she wasn't getting out of this house without having at least one cup of tea. It was Ellen's go-to for whatever ailed a person, and Laura had to admit it usually worked. She didn't think it was going to help tonight, though.

While she waited for the water to boil, Ellen sent a text message, which Laura assumed was to somebody at the garden club to let them know they wouldn't be there. Giving in to the inevitable, Laura clutched her cardigan around her and sat in the chair.

She was so cold. Maybe the tea would help with that, at least.

The first sip sent warmth through her, but it didn't last. She'd just have to keep sipping, she thought as Ellen sat across the table from her and waited. There were very few people more stubborn than a Sutton woman, so Laura forced herself to say the words.

"Riley and I are done."

Ellen actually looked stricken. "Oh, honey. I'm sorry. What happened?"

"It was too complicated. It's over now and that's that."

Ellen's gaze was locked on her, and Laura could see she didn't buy her attempt at a casual tone at all. "What was complicated?"

"Everything." Laura took a sip of her tea. She thought Ellen would be happy to have her other Lucy back. Lucy and Lucy would ride again. "I guess we'll have plenty of time for those adventures now."

Setting her mug of tea on the table, Ellen stared at her, disbelief and dismay written all over her face. "Laura Thompson, do *not* tell me you ended your relationship because I was feeling sorry for myself."

"No, I ended my relationship because there was *so much*. Our friendship means more to me than anything. His mother wants him to find a nice girl to give him sons, and at some point, he'll probably want that, too. It makes things awkward for Lane and Case. It's just easier for everybody if we end it now, before it gets messier."

"You mean before you fall any more in love with him."

"Yeah."

Ellen's eyes filled up with tears and one spilled over onto her cheek. "No, honey. You can't live your life for us. You were so happy. He was happy. You grab on to that and you don't let go."

Laura wished she could cry with her friend, but she wasn't sure she had any tears left in her. She'd cried them all out last night when she should have been sleeping. "I can't ignore the people I love being unhappy so I *can* be."

"I'm so sorry. I was just… I was feeling sorry for myself. It takes time when things change. But our friendship survived your husband dying. Our children divorcing. My husband dying. Our children finding their way back to each other. It would certainly have survived you falling in love."

"It wasn't just you, Ellen."

"Lane and Case work just fine with Riley. They're getting used to the personal aspect, but they *are* getting used to it. And as for Riley's mother? She'll get over it. You deserve to be happy."

"I'm terrified I'll lose myself again," she confessed. "You know how it was with Joe. I was Joe's wife and Lane's mom and the business bookkeeper. There was no *me*."

"You've grown so much stronger since Joe died. I don't think you could lose yourself if you tried."

And, dammit, she did have more tears in her. Laura's body shook as they ran down her face, and Ellen walked around the table to stand behind her and wrap her arms around her shoulders.

"Do you really love him?" she asked softly. Laura couldn't speak, so she nodded. "Then you keep him. I'll happily be your third wheel, and if his mother has a problem with it, you tell her she can stop by here anytime and talk to me about it."

A giggle bubbled up through the sobs. "I love him so much."

"I've had the great love of my life. I lost him, but I had so many years loving him with my whole heart. I want that for you. I love you, and I want you to have the love David and I had." Ellen stroked her hair. "I know you loved Joe, but it was different. Even back then, David and I knew that. Don't give up the chance for an epic love story because I had a pity party and his mother can't manage her expectations for her son's life."

"I don't want to come between them."

"Her relationship with her son is her problem. And if Riley has to choose between making his mother happy or making himself happy, that's *his* choice to make. Not yours."

"Ouch."

Ellen squeezed her shoulders and then went back to her seat so she could sip her tea. "I'll always tell you the hard truths because I love you. You know that."

Laura stretched her arm across the table and Ellen did the same, so their hands met in the middle. "I do know that. I hope you know I love you, too, and nothing and nobody can change that."

"I know." After squeezing fingers, they both picked up their tea and took long swallows. Maybe she was right about the tea, Laura thought. "And you know what? We're not getting any younger. These houses certainly aren't. As far as I'm concerned, the more strong young men we can trap into being part of the family, the better."

Laura's laughter surprised her, and it felt so good. "That's a valid point. I'll use that in my argument for why he should forgive me and take me back."

"If he loves you, you won't need to argue why."

The *if* echoed around in her head, making her chest hurt. Such a big, vital word made from those two little letters.

Chapter Twenty-One

The Perkin' Up Café will be closed next Tues-day through Thursday so upgrades can be done to the electrical wiring. Chelsea Grey tells us her fridge at home isn't very big, so from now until she closes on Monday, any beverage con-taining a perishable ingredient (milk, cream, some flavorings, etc.) will be 50 percent off. Take advantage of the sale to get your caffeine fix, folks, because those three days are going to feel endless!

—Stonefield Gazette *Facebook Page*

Riley showed up. He did his job. He went home to his tiny apartment with the aggressively cheerful yellow walls.

He made a turkey sandwich. Took three bites and threw it away. Sent a call from his mother to voice mail. Didn't listen to it. He scrolled through the TV's on-screen guide three times before turning it off. He tried to read, but it made him think of the evenings he'd spent reading to Laura, and he closed the book.

After pacing the length of the room several times and cursing more than a few times, he put his wallet and keys in his pocket, grabbed his phone and went for a walk. He hadn't intended to walk to Sutton's Place, but he wasn't surprised when he ended up at the taproom.

Irish set a coaster and a glass of dark beer in front of him as he slid onto a stool that was at the empty end of the bar. "New porter we're working on. You look like you could use something with a kick."

Kick it had, and he downed a third of it in one long swallow. "It's good."

Irish nodded. "Mostly Lane's recipe, though I made some suggestions. You want anything to eat?"

He should eat something. Too much beer after a couple of bites of a sandwich wasn't going to make him feel great in the morning. But it didn't matter. He wasn't going to feel great, anyway, because he was going to wake up thinking about Laura. He'd work all day thinking about Laura. Then he'd go home and think about Laura.

"No, I'm good."

"No offense, but you don't *look* good."

Riley shrugged. "You win some, you lose some."

Then he downed more beer as Irish walked away. He watched the cowboy pick up his phone and send a text message before sliding it into his back pocket and going back to his customers.

Riley assumed he was talking to Mallory, but twenty minutes later, Lane walked in and Irish nodded in Riley's direction.

Great. Just what he needed.

Lane slid onto the stool next to his, and Irish set a pale ale in front of him before leaving them alone.

Riley figured getting fired would just be the cherry on the misery sundae. "Good porter. This is my second."

"Thanks. And did Irish tell you the ABV is on the high side?"

He shrugged a shoulder. "I walked here."

"Irish told me you were here, and I figured it might be a good time for us to talk."

"Sure." It wasn't as if his night could get any worse. Losing his job didn't feel like that big a deal after losing Laura.

"I don't know where to start." Lane took a long swallow of the ale.

Your relationship with my mother went sideways, and we don't want to see you around, so you're fired. It wasn't that hard.

"My mom has always been a light in my life," Lane said finally, which wasn't what Riley had expected to hear. "She was the light waiting for me at the end of the tunnel. My North Star. The outside light shining in the dark. The lighthouse warning me off the rocks. Her light has been a constant in my life."

"She's that kind of woman," Riley said when he paused, not knowing what else to say.

"I've been thinking about that word—*constant*— since we hired you and all this started."

Riley felt it coming—now Lane was going to fire him—but he kept his mouth shut. There was no cause, which meant it would be personal. Lane would fire him because of his relationship with Laura, and he was going to make the man say it out loud.

"When you came into our lives, I saw her start to…sparkle. I don't know if that's the right word, but I can't think of a better one. She sparkled, like sparklers on the Fourth of July, or fireworks. It was like she was a banked campfire for my entire life, just burning embers, and then all of a sudden there's this awesome campfire."

Okay, maybe he *wasn't* getting fired.

"I suck at this," Lane said, and then he took a long swallow of beer. "Look. I want my mom to feel what you made her feel. I don't want to hear about it. But I want her to feel it."

Riley cleared his throat. "It wasn't my call."

"I know. But I don't think my mom pushed you away because of you. I think it was because of my dad. I loved him. My mom loved him, too. But she got pregnant with me when she was seventeen, and her family… Well, all of a sudden she's got a husband and a baby. I don't know if Mom ever got to make a decision just for herself until twenty years later, when my dad passed away. Hell, I didn't even know she hates our house until recently."

Chuckling, Riley shook his head. "*Hate*'s a strong word, I think. But I've heard about the closed-in spaces and the lighting a few times."

"Looking back to when I was a kid, I think it goes even deeper than that. My dad didn't like pork."

"Laura loves pork chops."

"Yeah, she does. And she didn't eat them for twenty years. She watched shows she didn't like for twenty years. And my dad wasn't a jerk or anything. It was just a really old-fashioned dynamic, I think. He was the head of the household, so the household ran his way."

He stopped talking long enough so Riley felt as if he was expected to say something, but he didn't know what. There was no way he would give an opinion on Lane's parents' marriage. He just nodded and took another sip of his beer.

Lane took the hint. "Anyway, I guess what I'm trying to say is that after my dad died, my mom got to be…just Laura. I mean, Evie and I moved back into the house, but she was the mom and I was grown, so she didn't have to answer to anybody anymore. If she wanted a bowl of cereal for supper or leftover pork chops for breakfast, it was nobody's business but hers. And I think she's afraid of giving that up."

"I'd like to think Laura knows me better than that by now," Riley said, trying not to get his back up about it. "I don't care if she has leftover pork chops for breakfast. If I'm not in the mood for that—and look, I probably won't be—I can make myself whatever I want and sit with her while she eats them."

"It's not about you, though. It's just *her*. Like I said, my dad didn't demand things from her. It was just how things were—the household revolved around him—and I think he picked that up from my grandparents. So she's probably afraid if she tries again, it'll be so ingrained in her she won't be able to help it."

"I don't know how to make her trust it won't happen."

"I don't, either," Lane admitted. "I just wanted you to know it's not because she doesn't like you."

"I appreciate that." Riley looked over at him. "A little surprised you're telling me that, to be honest."

"It's weird—you and her. It might *always* be weird. I don't know." Lane chuckled and then grew serious again. "But now that I've seen my mom really sparkling, I can also see when she isn't."

It hurt to think about Laura not sparkling. It hurt so much Riley set his glass back on the bar because he didn't know if he could even swallow the liquid, or if he'd choke on it.

"I think she's scared, and I also think she's taking care of everybody else instead of herself. Ellen. Me."

"And me," Riley said after clearing his throat. "She thinks she'll come between me and my mom."

"I've always said my mother doesn't have a selfish bone in her body like it was a compliment—like that was one of the best things about her. I didn't realize until I saw her earlier that what that really means is that she'll sacrifice her own happiness to keep everybody else happy. I hope you won't let her do it without a fight."

"I know I should come up with some quip about resparking her fire—"

"Please don't."

"—but I had a crap night and a worse day, so I can't think of one."

"On that note, I'm out of here." Lane drained the rest of his ale. "You know if you work this out with my mom, there's like a one hundred percent chance Becca's going to call you Grandpa, right?"

Riley almost choked on his beer, and Lane laughed at him. "I hadn't really thought about that."

"I have. And it's kind of funny to imagine us all hanging out with the kids and you're getting called *Grandpa*."

He chuckled. "That *would* be funny. But also really cool. I think I'd be pretty good at it."

"My kid could definitely do worse," Lane said easily, surprising him. Then he slid off the stool and slapped Riley on the back. "I'm going to see you at work no matter what happens, but I do hope you two figure it out. And I know how much we pay you, so you can pay for my beer."

After he was gone, Riley decided not to empty his glass and ask for another. It was a good porter with a strong kick he liked, but it wasn't great on an empty stomach. He paid his tab and Lane's and left the change for Irish.

"Hey," the cowboy said as he prepared to leave. "I know it might be hard to believe, but we all liked you two together."

"Thanks. I did, too."

As he walked back to his apartment, Riley couldn't help but think about the night he'd walked home with Laura at his side, wishing he could hold her hand. Just being with her had made the night memorable, but he'd thought if they hadn't had to be a secret, it would have been one of the best nights of his life. Now they weren't a secret at all, and it had fallen apart.

Then he saw his truck in the driveway and remembered kissing her there, with her back pressed up against it. There was no way he was going to spend the rest of his life without her and not even try to put up a fight about it.

But they hadn't been kidding about the punch that porter packed, and he couldn't get behind the wheel of his truck. Even without the risk to his CDL, it would be a stupid thing to do.

He wasn't going to get another chance with Laura by making his case by text message or over the phone, though. All he could do for now was go to bed, try to hold the hope in his heart instead of the pain, and then tomorrow he would swing for the fences.

Laura was curled up in her porch chair, sipping her coffee, when the guys started arriving for the workday. She'd had a restless night, and had woken earlier than usual with her mind filled with things she wanted to say to Riley.

They'd have to wait. There was work to be done.

The door opened, and Lane stepped out onto the porch. He was wearing his work boots, and his good gloves were sticking out of the back pocket of his jeans. She frowned. "Are you working with the crews today?"

"Yeah. Riley called in sick, so I'm covering for him."

Laura's breath caught in her chest, and she set the coffee mug down on the side table because her hands were trembling all of a sudden and she didn't want it sloshing over her hands. "He's sick?"

Lane shrugged. "Evie's upstairs with Becca. She said she's going to declutter our closet this morning, so she'll be a while. I'll see you after work."

He walked away before she could say anything else. Evie hadn't said anything to her about her plans, but Laura had assumed she'd have things to do. Her plan for getting through the day involved Becca and spreadsheets. And having Becca would keep her from driving to Riley's place and seeing if he was really sick or not.

Maybe he was leaving the tree service, and he'd called in sick because he had an interview with another company. Maybe her fear that getting involved with him would screw over the company had come true.

She sat there, her thoughts racing in the worst directions, while the trucks pulled out. Then there were no distractions. No guys. No granddaughter. She'd even left her phone inside. There was nothing but silence and her own thoughts.

Until she heard the low rumble of a motorcycle and her heart skipped a beat. It grew closer, and maybe it was wishful thinking, but it sounded like Riley's. She told herself it was possible he'd shaken off whatever was ailing him and was showing up for work, anyway, a few minutes too late. But her pulse was racing, and when his bike came into view, she blew out a shuddering breath.

When he passed the lower driveway and turned the bike to park next to her car, tears welled in her eyes. He could be coming to tell her he'd found a new job and was leaving Stonefield. But he'd definitely come to see her, and thinking back over what Lane had said about his and Evie's morning plans, her son had known he was coming. She took a deep breath, trying to steady her nerves.

After setting his helmet on the seat of his bike, Riley walked up the steps. He didn't look at her. Instead, he picked up one of the other porch chairs and carried it over. He set it down so it was facing her and sat down.

And *then* he looked at her. That gaze, so warm and steady, locked with hers, and she felt as if she was drowning in the ocean blue-gray of them.

"Hey," he said, and the small, tired smile he gave her broke her heart all over again.

"Hey."

"I need you to block out all the other voices. There are a lot of them, but shut them out and just listen to *me* for a minute." He paused, taking a deep breath. "I love you, Laura. I want to share my life with you. That's all I want. And I don't want you to see everybody else. I want you to see *me*. You know me. And more importantly, you know that I see *you*. I know you and I love you. I love *us*."

"I love us, too, but…"

"But what? But I'll want kids someday? I have kids in my life—kids I can hand back to their parents when they're cranky, I might add. Lane told me if you and I can get through this, Becca will end up calling me Grandpa, and he thought it was funny, but it made me happy. I would love that so much."

She didn't know Lane had said that—that Lane and Riley had even spoken about it—and her throat felt tight with unshed tears. Riley was being honest— she could see it in his eyes—and she wanted that. She wanted to share the joy of being a grandparent with him.

"Or is it *but Ellen*?" he continued. "I know she's

used to having you all to herself and the adjustment's probably been hard, but she'll get used to me. And those adventures you two were looking forward to? Have them. Go on the cruise. I'll be here when you get back, waiting to hear all about it. Go to knitting club and book club and garden club. Go find yard sales with her. I don't need to be your sole focus. I don't *want* to be."

"Until you've had a long day at work, and you come home and there's no supper on the table because Ellen talked me into going to the yarn store in the city, and we lost track of time."

His expression softened. "If I come home after a long day at work and there's no supper on the table, I'll call up Stonefield House of Pizza and have them deliver. And I'll save you some, so when you get home, you can have a slice before you show me what you bought. Or you can put it in the fridge and eat it cold for breakfast the next morning, while I make myself some scrambled eggs."

She sighed because she could picture it so clearly, and she wanted that. She wanted it so badly her stomach hurt. And she believed him.

"You know me, Laura. You know I don't need you to take care of me. I don't care what shows we watch. I don't need you to cook for me or do my laundry. I've been taking care of myself for a long time, and so have you. I just want us to do it together. If being a wife and the legal contract and all that doesn't appeal to you again, I don't need a ring. I just want to be with you. That's all."

"And your family? Your mom?" She had to pause to swallow hard. "I don't want to come between you and your mother. I can't."

"You won't. Look, every family has a different dynamic. You and Lane have a certain kind of relationship, and so do my mom and I. She doesn't do well with change—with adjusting ideas she's had in her head—and she'll panic and say anything she needs to preserve those ideas. But then she adjusts and moves on."

"And she's going to move on from you having sons to continue the McLaughlin name?" She shook her head. "That's kind of a big one, Riley."

"So big she's never mentioned it before in my entire life. Meeting you made her realize she'd always just assumed I'd have kids someday, and the possibility I wouldn't threw her off. And since she already has five grandkids, the McLaughlin name was the only thing she could think of to grab on to. But it's not actually something she cares about, and once she's gotten used to the idea that I'm happy just as we are, she'll be fine."

"And if she's not?"

"I know my mom, and she *will* really like you. I promise." He shrugged. "And I feel like if I can navigate the town librarian having to send in his fiancée undercover to steal back a library book you decided you were going to just keep, you can navigate my mother's anxiety."

She laughed, shaking her head. "I wasn't going to keep it. It was just going to be extra late."

"Do you have any more *buts*?" he asked, his eyes growing serious again. "What else is holding you back?"

There was nothing. When she looked into his eyes, all she saw was the man she loved. And the only voice in her head was her own, telling her she could spend the rest of her life with him. All she had to do was trust in him—in *them*.

"Nothing," she said. "No more *buts*."

"I asked you to shut all those other voices out, but that was only for this moment. I'll never ask you to shut somebody out of your life, or to rearrange your relationship with them to suit me. You and I can have it all, together, but this moment right here is about what *you* want."

"I want you," she said without hesitation. "I want *us*. I love you, and I was going to tell you that after work today. I thought about what I wanted to say to you all night."

"I'll listen if you want to say it all now."

She smiled. "There was a lot of sorting through some fears, but we've already done that, so all that's left is that I love you and I want to spend the rest of my life with you."

It was a good thing she'd put her coffee cup down, because Riley reached across the distance between them and half lifted, half dragged her onto his lap. She straddled his thighs, a little breathless at the reminder of how strong he was.

He swiped the tears from her cheeks with his thumbs. "You and me. Forever."

"Forever," she whispered, and then his hand was on the back of her neck and his mouth was on hers, and everything was good in the world again.

He kissed her until she forgot the pain of the last two days and her own name and how to breathe. He kissed her until there was nothing but the two of them in this moment, loving each other.

Until a car driving by honked its horn, startling her. He chuckled when she jumped, and brushed some wisps of her hair from her face.

"Maybe we'll make the *Gazette*," he said, and she laughed, not caring if they did.

"I told Lane I wanted to find a place of my own," she said, still straddling his lap. Based on the way his hands were holding her hips, he didn't mind. "Maybe we find one together."

"I actually don't love living at a funeral home as much as one would think, so a little place of our own sounds perfect. Something bright—though maybe not yellow—and open. No shiplap, though. A couple of bedrooms." He grinned. "Or maybe three bedrooms. One for us, one for Becca's sleepovers and one for your yarn."

She laughed, slapping his arm. "I don't have *that* much yarn."

"Not yet, but you and Ellen talk about buying yarn a lot more than you talk about knitting, so I'm starting to wonder what the actual hobby is here."

"That's fair," she admitted. "Though just for that, I'm going to knit you the ugliest Christmas sweater you've ever seen."

"And I'll wear it everywhere we go." He grinned when she rolled her eyes. "And I'd like a dog."

"A dog would be nice."

"Honestly, I'd like to dognap Boomer, but that would make Thanksgivings and birthday barbecues super awkward, so it's probably better if we get our own dog."

"Probably. And we don't want the dog or the grand-kids running off, so a white picket fence would be a good idea."

He grinned at her. "That sounds perfect. I can't wait."

She pushed off of his lap and held out her hand. "Since you called in sick today, I guess I'd better tuck you into bed."

He took her hand and stood, but then he pulled her in for a quick, hard kiss. Then he ran his thumb over her bottom lip. "I love you, Laura Thompson."

"I love you, too, Riley McLaughlin. I've been waiting my whole life for you."

"I'm here now. And always."

Epilogue

Two years later

"Gramps! Push me!"

Laura grinned at Riley, who'd just settled into the porch rocker with an iced tea. "Hey, you got to sit for a whole thirty seconds this time."

"Gramps!" Becca yelled again, her voice surprisingly big for such a small little girl.

"Isn't it your turn to push her on the swing?"

Laura pointed to the sleeping bundle cradled in her right arm. Joey—Joseph David, for Lane's and Evie's fathers—was two months old and quite possibly the quietest baby she'd ever seen. She certainly wasn't complaining.

Riley waved at Becca, gesturing for her to come

over. She did so, at full speed because that was the only way she did anything, and leaned on his knee. Their chocolate Lab, Mocha, looked up from his shady spot under a tree, but didn't get up. He knew she'd be back.

"What, Gramps?"

"If you let me sit quietly on this porch with Nana until my iced tea is gone, I'll take you for ice cream after lunch."

She grinned, looking so much like Lane Laura's heart ached. "Mommy says you give me too much ice cream."

"Then Mommy can come push you on the swing."

Laura smothered a chuckle when Becca frowned. "But she's not here."

"I know, sweetie. Why don't you work on our rock garden for a little while, and after we eat, we'll go for ice cream."

Becca tore off to the rock garden, where she'd rearrange pretty rocks Riley found on jobs into towers and shapes until they were just the way she liked them. She loved being outdoors, and it gave them something to do together.

Laura watched her and then smiled at Riley before resting her head against the back of her rocking chair and sighing with contentment.

Life didn't get much better than this, she thought. The little house—or her cottage, as the others called it—still wasn't totally finished, but they'd moved in at the beginning of the summer, anyway. After bouncing between her house and his apartment while searching in vain for someplace they liked, they'd decided to build. They'd been able to subdivide Laura's—Lane's—property so Laura could take a small piece of the land on the other side of the house from the garage. They left a strip of woods so there was some privacy, but it was close enough so when Becca was a little older, she'd be able to walk over on the path they'd cut through the trees.

It was a simple floor plan. It was entirely open, except for the two bedrooms and bathroom. All windows and light, it made her happy just to walk through the front door. The guys had built it themselves, after work and on weekends, which meant it had taken a while. But it was exactly the way she wanted it. Plus, they'd calculated the cost of building it, and Lane and Evie had bought the big house for that amount. Lane continued leasing the garage to the tree service, so they all made out in the end.

"Nana!" Becca was coming, full tilt, with a rock in her hand. Laura had gotten pretty good at lifting her leg slightly so if her granddaughter crashed into her, she wouldn't jostle the baby.

"This one's a heart!" Becca exclaimed, holding it up so Laura could see it.

It did look like a heart, and she could see letters scratched into it. *R&L.* She looked at Riley, who grinned at her.

"I found that one last week. I knew one of you would find it eventually."

"What do the letters mean?" Becca asked, running her fingers over them.

"That's our names," Riley said. "*R* is for *Riley* and *L* is for *Laura*."

Becca gave him a look that clearly said she thought he was the silliest person on the planet. "Your name is Gramps. And Nana."

She was gone before he could explain, and he just chuckled and shook his head.

Laura remembered when Lane had first called Riley Gramps, meaning it as a joke. He and Case both thought it was hilarious to call their friend Gramps, and she had no idea if Becca picking it up was intentional or not on their parts, but it had stuck.

What they didn't realize was how much Riley loved the name. Being Becca's Gramps was one of the biggest joys in his life, and he'd mentioned more than once he was going to try to teach Joey to say it. He thought it would be a good first word for Lane's son.

"What time are they getting back?" Riley asked.

"Not until close to supper time," she said, and she laughed when he groaned.

"How about we trade? I'll sit here and hold the sleeping baby, and you keep up with Hurricane Becca. I swear, I don't know how Ellen survives with three little ones."

"Hers are spread across three kids, so she rarely has all three of them at once. And you'll notice how often Becca stays with Nana and not Grammy."

"I have noticed that." He took a swallow of iced tea and then smiled, watching their granddaughter trying to pile two big rocks on top of a small one. "I don't mind, though."

Especially since, a few hours from now, they'd give the kids back to their parents and send Mocha with them for the evening. Then she and Riley were going to get on the bike and go visit his parents. There would be too much food and a lot of laughter—because once she'd gotten over her surprise, Kris had come to adore Laura, as Riley had known she would—and hopefully his sisters would stop by with the kids. Then they'd take a different road home. Mocha would come when he heard the bike pull into their driveway. They'd maybe watch a little TV or read, and then they'd make love under the moon shining through the skylights in their bedroom.

They'd made a perfect life together.

"Hey," she said as the baby stirred slightly. When Riley turned to face her, she looked into his ocean-colored eyes and felt the love envelop her as always. "I love you."

"Still?"

"Always," she said.

His grin still took her breath away. "Good, because you read an awful lot of those dead-husband books, and I don't want you getting any ideas. Just because we're not married doesn't mean you can't murder me the same way they do."

"If I murder you, I'll have to handle both kids on

my own, though." She laughed. "I'm definitely going to keep you around."

He chuckled and then his gaze warmed. "And, hey, I love you, too."

* * * * *

#3001 THE MAVERICK'S SWEETEST CHOICE
Montana Mavericks: Lassoing Love • by Stella Bagwell

Rancher Dale Dalton only planned to buy cupcakes from the local bakery. Yet one look at single mom Kendra Humphrey and it's love at first sight. Or at least lust. Kendra wants more than a footloose playboy for her and her young daughter. But Dale's full-charm offensive may be too tempting and delicious to ignore!

#3002 FAKING A FAIRY TALE
Love, Unveiled • by Teri Wilson

Bridal editor Daphne Ballantyne despises her coworker Jack King. But when a juicy magazine assignment requires going undercover as a blissfully engaged couple, both Daphne and Jack say "I do." If only their intense marriage charade wasn't beginning to feel a lot like love...

#3003 HOME FOR THE CHALLAH DAYS
by Jennifer Wilck

Sarah Abrams is home for Rosh Hashanah...but can't be in the same room as her ex-boyfriend. She broke Aaron Isaacson's heart years ago and he's still deeply hurt. Until targeted acts of vandalism bring the reluctant duo together. And unearth buried—and undeniable—attraction just in time for the holiday.

#3004 A CHARMING DOORSTEP BABY
Charming, Texas • by Heatherly Bell

Dean Hunter's broken childhood still haunts him. So there's no way the retired rodeo star will let his neighbor Maribel Del Toro call social services on a mother who suddenly left her daughter in Maribel's care. They'll *both* care for the baby...and maybe even each other.

#3005 HER OUTBACK RANCHER
The Brands of Montana • by Joanna Sims

Hawk Bowhill's heart is on his family's cattle ranch in Australia. But falling for fiery Montana cowgirl Jessie Brand leads to a bevy of challenges, and geography is the least of them. From two continents to her unexpected pregnancy to her family's vow to keep them apart, will the price of happily-ever-after be too high to pay?

#3006 HIS UNLIKELY HOMECOMING
Small-Town Sweethearts • by Carrie Nichols

Shop owner Libby Taylor isn't fooled by Nick Cabot's tough motorcycle-riding exterior. He helped her daughter find her lost puppy...and melted Libby's guarded emotions in the process. But despite Nick's tender, heroic heart, can she take a chance on love with a man convinced he's unworthy of it?

HSECNM0723

Get 3 FREE REWARDS!

We'll send you 2 FREE Books plus a FREE Mystery Gift.

FREE Value Over **$20**

Both the **Harlequin® Special Edition** and **Harlequin® Heartwarming™** series feature compelling novels filled with stories of love and strength where the bonds of friendship, family and community unite.

YES! Please send me 2 FREE novels from the Harlequin Special Edition or Harlequin Heartwarming series and my FREE Gift (gift is worth about $10 retail). After receiving them, if I don't wish to receive any more books, I can return the shipping statement marked "cancel." If I don't cancel, I will receive 6 brand-new Harlequin Special Edition books every month and be billed just $5.49 each in the U.S. or $6.24 each in Canada, a savings of at least 12% off the cover price, or 4 brand-new Harlequin Heartwarming Larger-Print books every month and be billed just $6.24 each in the U.S. or $6.74 each in Canada, a savings of at least 19% off the cover price. It's quite a bargain! Shipping and handling is just 50¢ per book in the U.S. and $1.25 per book in Canada.* I understand that accepting the 2 free books and gift places me under no obligation to buy anything. I can always return a shipment and cancel at any time by calling the number below. The free books and gift are mine to keep no matter what I decide.

Choose one: ☐ **Harlequin Special Edition** (235/335 BPA GRMK)   ☐ **Harlequin Heartwarming Larger-Print** (161/361 BPA GRMK)   ☐ **Or Try Both!** (235/335 & 161/361 BPA GRPZ)

Name (please print)

Address   Apt. #

City   State/Province   Zip/Postal Code

Email: Please check this box ☐ if you would like to receive newsletters and promotional emails from Harlequin Enterprises ULC and its affiliates. You can unsubscribe anytime.

Mail to the **Harlequin Reader Service:**
IN U.S.A.: P.O. Box 1341, Buffalo, NY 14240-8531
IN CANADA: P.O. Box 603, Fort Erie, Ontario L2A 5X3

Want to try 2 free books from another series! Call 1-800-873-8635 or visit www.ReaderService.com.

HARLEQUIN
PLUS

Try the best multimedia subscription service for romance readers like you!

Read, Watch and Play.

Experience the easiest way to get the romance content you crave.

Start your **FREE TRIAL** at
www.harlequinplus.com/freetrial.